"Married?"

His ruthlessly beautiful mouth twisting, he said, "If you're conscience-stricken because you've been unfaithful to the saintly Michael, let me remind you he's been dead for almost three years. It's time you let him go."

She shook her head, searching through her mind for memories of a dead husband and finding only echoing, empty caverns "Who are you?" she asked again, her words strained and desperate.

Contempt gleamed in his half-closed eyes. "Stop it now—it's not working," he said softly, lethally. "I'm the only man you made love with last night, the man whose arms you slept in."

Unable to meet that probing gaze, she dropped her face into her hands. "I don't know who you are," she blurted unevenly, trying to flog her aching brain into producing a memory. When it remained obstinately and terrifyingly empty she wailed, "I don't even know who I am. I don't know where this is. I don't know—I don't know anything!"

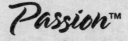

Robyn Donald

FORGOTTEN SINS

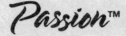

Passion™

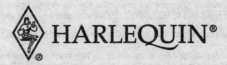

TORONTO • NEW YORK • LONDON
AMSTERDAM • PARIS • SYDNEY • HAMBURG
STOCKHOLM • ATHENS • TOKYO • MILAN • MADRID
PRAGUE • WARSAW • BUDAPEST • AUCKLAND

ISBN 0-373-12300-0

FORGOTTEN SINS

First North American Publication 2003.

Copyright © 2001 by Robyn Donald.

This edition published by arrangement with Harlequin Books S.A.

® and TM are trademarks of the publisher. Trademarks indicated with ® are registered in the United States Patent and Trademark Office, the Canadian Trade Marks Office and in other countries.

Visit us at www.eHarlequin.com

Printed in U.S.A.

CHAPTER ONE

JAKE saw Aline Connor the moment he walked into the drawing-room. Heat and desire hit him like a blow, bringing his body alive and nearly overpowering his confident self-possession.

How the hell, he thought with savage self-mockery, did she do that to him? Witchcraft?

He'd had a pig of a week, culminating in a delayed, turbulent flight from Canada to New Zealand the previous night, yet one glance and he knew he'd have travelled ten times as far to see her.

'Ah, there's the guest of honour,' cooed Lauren Penn, who'd pulled up outside the old Victorian villa at the same time as Jake, and strolled in with him. 'She's such a little darling, isn't she? Wasn't she good in the church—not a murmur as the vicar splashed her forehead! I think she's inherited Keir's massive self-assurance, lucky little girl.'

An undercurrent in her voice caught Jake's attention. Meeting his swift scrutiny with a sideways glance and a challenging smile, she used the doorway as an excuse to brush against him. Perfume, overtly erotic, rose in a clinging, cloying cloud; neither it nor the swift friction of skin against skin when she touched his hand affected Jake.

He'd grown cynical since he'd begun to appear in the eligible bachelor lists; certain women—those whose main aim in life was to fascinate a rich man into marriage—had targeted him. Although some had inspired casual desire, it had been nothing like the violent, elemental hunger he felt whenever he looked at Aline—or whenever he thought of her, or heard her, or touched her...

It had to be witchcraft, a spell spun by a black-haired,

5

blue-eyed witch with a voice like cool music and skin so silkily transparent he wondered whether it would show bruises after making love.

His mouth curled sardonically. In spite of her aloofness and reserve, he'd sensed a reluctant, involuntary response, but it clear as hell irked her, and it certainly wasn't anything as strong as the basic need that clawed through him.

Not that Aline's aloofness was personal; she didn't target anyone. Lauren Penn displayed more overt welcome in one smile than Aline showed in her whole graceful, elegant body. Yet from the moment he'd seen her he'd wanted her with a raw, consuming hunger that had nothing to do with logic or intelligence. Until then always able to control his passions, it angered and astonished him that he couldn't do it now.

Lauren sent him another melting glance and murmured, 'They look such a happy group, don't they? Aline cuddling baby Emma while Hope sits proudly by. Hope strikes me as the possessive sort, so all those rumours about Aline being Keir's lover can't be true.'

It wasn't the first time Jake had heard that particular suggestion, although usually as innuendo. It had angered him previously; it enraged him now. He liked Lauren, and if he hadn't heard a feverish note buried in her brittle words he wouldn't have bothered to silence his cutting response.

Something was clearly going on. It concerned Aline— and that meant it concerned him.

Lauren's gaze was fixed on Aline. Without waiting for an answer she drawled, 'Aline's cold-blooded enough to swap passion for friendship if it worked to her advantage, but I don't think Hope would welcome her husband's discarded lover as a friend.'

One of the reasons Jake hated the insinuation was that he suspected it had some basis; he'd sensed a certain tension between Keir Carmichael and his tall, exquisite executive, but he knew men—whatever had happened in the past, Keir wasn't interested in Aline now. Although his face made granite look expressive, he couldn't hide the way he felt about his wife.

Just as well, Jake thought with cold purposefulness. If he'd wanted Aline, Carmichael would have had a fight on his hands.

'Champagne, madam? Sir?' a waiter offered smoothly.

'Oh, lovely—perfect for such a glorious day,' Lauren accepted eagerly, her hand shaking as she took the glass. She raised it to Jake. 'I love spring—all those new beginnings make you glad to be alive, don't they?'

Every sense alert, Jake took a glass too, listening with half an ear as she delivered a rapid, amusing commentary on several other guests, infuriated when he caught himself glancing above her head at the woman who haunted him.

Poised, slender body disposed on a big sofa, patrician face alight, Aline Connor smiled at the baby in her lap. For the past two months she'd been negotiating with him on behalf of Keir Carmichael's merchant bank, displaying an intelligence sharp enough to keep Jake on his toes, disciplined enough to almost convince him of her indifference. Almost...

Beside her, Keir Carmichael's glowing wife, the mother of the baby, said something that set both women laughing. Laughing with them, the baby reached out chubby fingers to pat Aline's cheek. She caught the little hand and kissed it.

A shaft of pure sensation stabbed Jake with ferocious impact.

From beside him Lauren said with brittle intensity, 'I'm surprised to see Emma so happy in Aline's lap. I know Aline doesn't like children—she refused to have any when she was married to Mike, and he really wanted them.'

Jake had good instincts, and by now they were on full alert.

He lifted an intimidating eyebrow and glanced down at the woman beside him. She held her glass to her mouth like a shield; above the rim, her eyes were shiny and opaque.

Neutrally he said, 'I hadn't realised you knew them both so well.'

Her shoulders sketched a shrug. 'Aline was in my class at school.' Deepening her voice to add emphasis to her next words, she went on, 'She was the classic nerd—a skinny, conceited kid who never forgot to do her homework and scored top marks year after year until she took them for granted. I was the class clown and she despised me.' Lauren directed a wry look upwards, making clever use of long curling lashes. 'Not that I blame her—children are cruel, and we were awful to her.' She sipped more champagne before saying with a slow smile, 'Mind you, that was over twenty years ago and we *were* only kids.'

The implication being that Aline never forgot grudges, no matter how old and insignificant?

Negligently Jake observed, 'Did you go to school with her husband too?'

A fugitive emotion flashed over her exquisitely made-up face; Lauren took another, longer sip of champagne and shook her head. 'No, he was three years older than me, and went to a different school. His death was such a tragedy. We were all shattered.' Her glance stabbed across the room. 'I admired Aline enormously; she didn't cry at the funeral even though it must have been hell for her.'

The implication being that Aline hadn't cared much about her husband...?

Grimly aware that he'd have cut this conversation off before it had started if he hadn't been obsessed by its subject, Jake said, 'I'd heard it was a great romance.'

Lauren's face froze. For a second he saw malice and a dreadful bitterness in the wide eyes before they were hidden by those curling lashes.

'So everyone says,' she agreed tonelessly. 'Which is why I find it so difficult to believe that she was sleeping with Keir within a year of Mike's death.'

Her blind smile setting off more alarm signals, she continued brightly, 'It doesn't fit into the grieving widow scenario at all, does it? And then, of course, Mike...'

'Mike?' Jake probed, trying to keep his voice mildly interested, and failing. A faint rasp to his words betrayed his interest.

After a swift, furtive glance, Lauren veiled her eyes and stretched her mouth into a dazzling smile. 'Nothing important. But most men find being married to a snow queen pretty depressing. Oh, there's someone I have to say hello to! I'll see you later, Jake.' And, waving to an elderly man on the verandah, she set off across the room fast enough to suggest her departure was a definite escape.

Frowning, he watched as she embraced her quarry—Tony Hudson, a famous athlete of forty years previously, esteemed now for his work with at-risk children. Because of that Michael Connor had appointed him one of the trustees of his charitable trust, set up before his death and hugely supported by New Zealanders, one of whom was Jake's personal assistant.

His frown deepening, Jake drank some of the excellent champagne without tasting it. Lauren had looked off balance enough to cause a scene.

That hadn't worried him too much; his deliberate probing did. He didn't normally pump women—especially not social butterflies with bigger hair than brains—but he was becoming absurdly sensitive about Aline Connor.

And not because she refused to allow herself to be susceptible to him. His mouth tightened, then relaxed into a smile as his host came towards him. He didn't want a woman who was impressed by his wealth and power, but, with the ruthless, unsparing honesty that had made him more enemies than friends, he acknowledged that he wouldn't object in the least if Aline succumbed to this inconvenient attraction smouldering between them.

For all her wary reserve, she felt *something*; he could see her now, taking such care not to look across the room that her awareness of him pulsed around her like an aura. Well, they'd signed the deal a week ago. From now on they met as man and woman, not as business associates.

Keir said, 'Good that you could make it, Jake.'

Smiling, Jake shook hands. 'Your daughter is the most accomplished flirt I know; I wasn't going to miss her christening.'

Even before she saw him come in the door, Aline knew when Jake Howard arrived. His presence charged the atmosphere, sending out vibrations that homed in on her nerve-ends and caused swift chaos. Although she tried not to react, she stole a glance towards the door just in time to see him coming in with Lauren Penn.

Dark jealousy shafted through her. Shocked and startled by its force and depth, Aline tightened her grip around the baby in her lap, wishing that for once she'd left her hair loose so that she could hide behind it.

Emma squirmed. 'It's all right,' Aline soothed, releasing her. 'There, see, you're fine.'

The baby smiled forgivingly at her, revealing what looked like a tiny grain of rice on her lower gum.

'Sweetheart!' Aline exclaimed. 'You're getting a tooth! Aren't you too young?'

From across the room, Jake's scrutiny sent a familiar surge of anticipation and apprehension through her.

Hope said, 'Most babies start to teethe around six months, so she's right on target.'

'I don't know much about babies,' Aline said regretfully.

'You're doing very well with that one,' Hope said with a quick grin. 'Emma adores you.'

Emma chose that moment to give an elaborate yawn, and both women laughed. The baby smiled up at Aline and reached up to pat her cheek; Aline's heart melted. She kissed the chubby starfish hand. 'And I adore her.' Something compelled her to add, 'And *not* because she looks like Keir. That was a crazy stupidity I've recovered from.'

'I know.' Hope looked at her with warm empathy. 'Don't keep apologising, Aline. We've agreed to let it lie in the past where it belongs.'

Aline touched the baby's fine hair, cupping her hand protectively around the nape of her neck. 'I just wish it had never happened,' she said, sombre and intense. Driven and desperately unhappy, Aline had acted totally out of character by trying to break Hope's engagement. 'It didn't mean a thing to either of us. And I so wish I hadn't told you.'

'It doesn't *matter*.' Hope said firmly.

A glance at her face revealed that she was being completely truthful. Hope was so confident of her husband's love that a one-night stand before he met her again meant nothing.

She finished by saying, 'Forget it. I have.'

'You haven't, but you've certainly forgiven.' Pale and severe, Aline said, 'Which I don't deserve.'

'It's time you forgave yourself,' Hope said sternly. 'That's your problem, you know—you're a perfectionist, and you expect impossibly high standards from yourself. It's probably what makes you such an asset to Keir's bank, but it must be hell for you to live with.'

Aline said, 'It's the way I am.' She glanced from beneath her lashes across the room. Jake and Keir were talking, their combined masculinity overpowering.

Following her gaze, Hope observed with dry amusement, 'They should wear labels—"Caution, Dangerous Male". All we need is for Leo Dacre to join them, and every woman in the room would faint.' She hesitated, then asked, 'What do you think of Jake?'

Aline almost surrendered to her instincts and uttered the explosive character analysis that hovered on her tongue. Instead, perhaps she could ease some of the guilt she still felt at trying to prevent Hope and Keir's marriage.

With a smile she tried to purge of irony, she said, 'He's really something, isn't he?'

Hope said, 'He's gorgeous.'

But her eyes lingered on her husband, not on Jake. For Hope no other man existed but Keir. Once Aline had felt like that too, but Michael was dead.

She stirred, transferring her gaze to Emma, who was solemnly watching the crowd assembled in her honour. If Michael hadn't wanted to wait for children, Aline might be holding her own child...

Banishing the painful thought, she said crisply, 'Got it in one. Jake Howard is gorgeous.'

Her hostess gave a snort of laughter. 'Actually, that's the wrong word. "Gorgeous" makes me think of sleek, pouting male models, all biceps and bravado. Jake's got classic features.' Her glance switched to Aline. 'Like you, in fact. And, like you, he has a formidable brain.'

When Aline pulled a face, Hope went on quietly, 'Though I know you've had to fight for the right to be taken seriously—life's not fair for clever women, especially when they're beautiful.'

'At least I'm not blonde—they find it even more difficult,' Aline said.

Ironic that she'd happily, swiftly, surrender her cool, lifeless, regular features for a tenth of the warmth and fire and individuality that blazed from Hope.

Hope said thoughtfully, 'I wonder if Jake's wonderful face means that the strength and intelligence behind it was overlooked when he started building his empire? I bet lots of people dismissed him as just a handsome lightweight.'

'I'm sure he'd have turned it to his advantage. By the time they realised he's about as lightweight as Mount Ruapehu he'd probably taken them over,' Aline pointed out, reluctantly recalling her first impression of Jake Howard.

Well-briefed, she'd known that he'd used his brilliant degree to set up as a forestry consultant straight out of university. Within ten years he'd built a huge organisation with global interests, and a reputation for fairness and honesty—and ruthlessness when he was attacked. She'd read about his takeovers, and the way he'd cut ethnic minorities in as stakeholders in his projects.

Yet when she'd first met him it had been his sheer physical presence and his potent, lethal sexuality that had slammed through her barriers.

Hope said cheerfully, 'Keir says he's got discipline and daring, and enough focus and determination to take over the world if he wants to.' She laughed again. 'And he's good with babies too. Emma bats her lashes and coos at him. He should get married and raise a dynasty.'

'All he'd have to do is wave a wedding ring,' Aline snapped, adding lamely, 'Anyway, he might have girls instead of sons.'

Hope's brows lifted. 'So? You're living proof that women can make it in the world of business.'

'Ah, but I was my father's son,' Aline told her, her mouth twisting.

'He must have been proud of you.'

Relaxing her rigid shoulders, Aline pinned on a smile. 'I hope so,' she said, glancing surreptitiously past the baby to where Jake and Keir had been joined by Lauren, all flicking hair and sultry seduction.

Jake looked up. For long, timeless seconds their eyes clashed, duelling across the room.

He radiated energy—a formidable, hypnotic power that sent shivery chills up her spine. Nothing like Michael,

who'd been big-hearted and gallant and joyous—and
who'd died. Why did death take the best?

Deliberately she broke contact, only to meet Lauren's
gaze; the woman lifted a glass of champagne to her, her
smile glittering. Aline forced her lips into an answering
curve, grateful when Emma leapt excitedly in her arms,
almost overbalancing. Hauling her back to safety, she said
crisply, 'Emma's not the only one who flirts with Jake.'

'No.' Hope's voice was troubled. 'Something's been
hounding Lauren for years, but it looks as though she's
getting really close to the edge. Her father's so worried
about her.'

With the confidence of a child who has known nothing
but love, Emma raised a commanding hand, worked her
mouth earnestly, and eventually produced a sound so close
to *boo* that both women laughed, and Aline forgot
Lauren's hostility.

In a few minutes she allowed herself another glance
across the room to see Lauren flirting with another young
man, Keir charming a pleasant middle-aged woman, and
Jake talking—no, listening—to an earnest Tony Hudson,
one of the trustees of Michael's charitable trust.

Making a mental note to contact Tony again this week
and try again to persuade him it was time the trust gave
some of its millions of dollars to the young people it was
set up to help, Aline relaxed.

But when the hair on the back of her neck stood up in
primitive recognition of danger, she knew without raising
her eyes who'd joined them. Right in front of her she saw
long legs and narrow hips, a man's confident, almost aggressive stance.

Thank heavens Jake's negotiations with the bank were
over; from now on others would deal with him and his
business. She'd no longer wake each morning haunted by
the challenge in his dark face, the special note in his voice

that reached right down inside her, taunting her with her hidden weakness.

Keeping her head down, she dropped a kiss on the baby's satin cheek.

Beside her Hope said, 'Jake! How lovely to see you!'

'How do you manage to glow like that?' The practised compliment came easily, but there was no doubt about the pure male appreciation in his voice.

Emma bounced and launched herself forwards, holding out chubby arms with a smile that almost split her face.

'Well, button, is that a tooth I see?' Jake's voice came closer as he dropped onto his haunches and touched the baby's cheek.

Startled, Aline looked into tawny-gold eyes—eagle's eyes, she'd thought at their first meeting, piercing and merciless. Subsequent meetings hadn't changed her mind.

He smiled crookedly at her. 'Hello, Aline.'

A flutter of pulse at the base of her throat drew his gaze; weighed down by the laughing baby, Aline couldn't drag her eyes from his face. He was so close she could see the small laughter lines fanning out from the corners of those relentless eyes, the thick black lashes, and the chiselled, beautiful lines of his mouth with its thinner upper lip and disturbingly curved lower.

Always before she'd avoided his scrutiny by focusing just past him; now, her head spinning, her senses afire, she drowned in gold. Something had altered. She sensed a difference in Jake, a deeply dominant shift in attitude.

With an effort of will that took all her strength, she deliberately shut down her treacherous awareness, withdrawing into the guarded fastness only Michael had been able to enter.

Jake's mouth curved in mocking recognition of her silent rejection. He got to his feet with a lithe grace that proclaimed power and control. 'Here, give the heroine of the day to me,' he said, reaching out confident arms.

Transferring a chuckling baby meant that Aline had to get much closer, had to touch him for the first time except when they'd shaken hands—something she'd tried to limit, only to have him force the gesture every time they'd met and parted.

Her heart thudded painfully; without looking at him she settled Emma into his iron embrace and stepped back, ambushed by the heat radiating from him, and his hard, tensile masculinity.

All right, she told herself as the conversation was taken over efficiently by the others, *admit* it. You are—you're *aware* of him.

The last honest part of her brain sniggered and drawled, To put it bluntly, you want him. Even more bluntly, you want to go to bed with him.

Well, why not? It was merely a ruthlessly physical 'Me Tarzan, you Jane' response, carefully formulated by Mother Nature to perpetuate the species. He was all alpha male, while she was a woman in her late twenties with her biological clock beginning to tick.

She hated being so vulnerable to Jake Howard's intense magnetism, his elemental strength and determination. Her weakness betrayed everything she'd felt for her husband because not even Michael had delivered such a blazing punch of erotic excitement.

But she'd shared much more with Michael; he'd valued her for many other things besides her femaleness.

Every time Jake looked at her she saw recognition of her as a sexual being in those eagle's eyes, in the way he spoke and responded to her. Even when they'd been negotiating hard and forcefully he'd made sure she knew he liked what he saw.

And his tactics had worked. Now her skin tightened whenever he came into a room, his presence invading her guarded detachment.

Hope laughed as he tossed Emma into the air. 'You can

do that all day and she'll still want more—she has a cast-iron stomach. You're very experienced with children.'

'I like them,' he said simply. 'Nice basic things, kids. You know exactly where you are with them—if they don't like you they howl and struggle; if they decide you're a fit person to hold them they smile and coo.' His glinting eyes moved to Aline's face. 'There's no wasting time with children; they won't allow it.'

Hope's brows shot up, but she returned a remark that made him laugh, and then Keir arrived, and for five minutes or so they chatted with relaxed ease.

Too soon, but inevitably, Hope and Keir moved on, taking Emma with them. With her usual store of small talk evaporating fast, Aline cast around for something innocuous to say before escaping.

Jake watched her from beneath his lashes, an unnerving glint of mockery lighting his eyes.

Edgily she summoned a cool smile. 'I didn't realise you were going to be here,' she said, hoping the observation didn't sound as inane to him as it did to her.

Her hope was dashed immediately. 'You mean you assumed I wouldn't be. Do you want me to go?'

'No!' She inhaled quickly, sharply, to settle her racing pulses. 'Of course not,' she said, encouraged when her voice revealed nothing more than polite interest.

She lifted her eyes, only to find them captured by his. Dazedly, she felt as though she'd fallen into frozen fire, lost all individuality, all reason, all control...

Forcing another tight smile, she went on, 'I thought you were in Vancouver,' and wrenched her gaze free of the forbidden imprisonment of his, fixing her eyes on his mouth.

Only to discover that it was as dangerous to her peace of mind as his tawny-gold eyes. Sex, she reminded herself sturdily, that's all it is. Yes, it was humiliating to be attracted to a man like Jake, a man so unlike Michael they had almost nothing in common except their gender, but she'd get over it now she didn't have to see him so often.

'Jets leave Canada every day for New Zealand. I plan to be seeing quite a bit of Keir and his wife in the future.'

'They're a lovely family,' Aline said tautly.

Silence stretched between them, buzzing with hidden significance. He waited, but when she refused to break it he said with smooth insolence, 'And I plan to be seeing more of you.'

She gave him a small, meaningless smile. 'I don't imagine we'll need to meet again now that we've stitched up the deal—'

'This has nothing to do with the deal.' He paused before saying in a voice underpinned by steel, 'This is about us, Aline. You and me.'

The drawing-room was large and filled with people, all at that pleasant state of talkativeness engendered by a glass of excellent champagne. More people had spilled out of the open French doors onto the wide Victorian verandah beyond. It bore the hallmarks of an excellent party, yet Aline sat alone, imprisoned by his inflexible will.

Hands clenched by her sides, she said, 'No,' the word a stone dropped into echoing silence.

Strong fingers closed around her wrist, shackling it. 'I can feel your heartbeat against my fingertips,' Jake said thoughtfully. 'It's going twice the normal speed.'

Before she tried to twist free he released her. 'No,' she said again, the meaningless word splintering into the tension between them. 'And don't ever do that again. I don't like being manhandled.'

From behind came a sly voice, soft, heavy with innuendo. 'She's never liked being touched. Except by her husband, of course,' Lauren Penn said. Her smile bubbled into laughter, low and mocking. 'And you know, that's a joke. Just the biggest joke in the world.'

'Lauren…' Aline's glance swerved to the half-empty glass of champagne in the other woman's hand.

Lauren swallowed the rest of the wine, setting the empty glass down with exaggerated care on a table. *'Lauren,'* she mimicked. 'Lauren, shut up. Lauren, go away. Lauren, stop making a scene. You know, I'm so sick of you. Ever since he died you've worn your grief for your darling lost Michael like a bloody crown. Other people grieved too, but that never occurred to you, did it?' Her glance darted to Jake's angular face.

As though encouraged by his dispassionate regard, she purred, 'You see, Jake, poor Aline has a little problem. She *really* doesn't like being touched—and that's straight from the horse's mouth. Mike said she was like turquoise, cold and smooth and shallow—nothing but surface colour. He called her the Untouchable—sometimes the Snow Queen. He said that when they had sex it was like worshipping at some shrine instead of loving a flesh-and-blood woman—'

'That's more than enough.' Jake's voice held such crackling menace that Lauren went white. Her eyes moved from Jake's grim face to Aline, locked in a hideous stasis.

Jake said softly, 'Get out of here.'

Lauren whispered, 'It's time she knew. She's eating her heart out for a lie. I loved Mike and he loved me. We'd been lovers for a year when he died.' Her eyes glazed with tears and her mouth trembled. 'He wanted to come away with me, but he didn't want to hurt her. We were going to get married.'

Unable to hold back, Aline retorted in a shaking voice, 'I don't believe you.'

'Because you don't want to.' Open antagonism sharpened her words. 'Do you know what happened when he died? I lost our baby.'

Her anguished glance across the room to Emma, smiling in her father's arms, struck both Jake and Aline mute.

Bitterly she went on, 'If you hadn't clung so hard he'd have left you, and then he and my baby would still be alive. *I* wouldn't have let him fly across the sea looking for some idiot solo yachtsman who'd got himself lost. You killed Mike—and you killed my baby because you wouldn't let go!'

That was when Aline knew she was telling the truth.

CHAPTER TWO

IT HURT, Aline realised, to breathe. It even hurt to think. The last time she could remember such pain was when they'd told her Michael was dead. The irony almost knocked her to her knees.

Lauren said softly, 'You're so stubborn and self-centred, so sure you're always right, but tomorrow you'll have to believe me. I even lent the author Mike's letters.'

Jake's eyes narrowed. 'What the hell are you talking about?' he asked in a tone that wilted Lauren's antagonism.

Defiantly she said, 'Aline refused to talk to the writer—Stuart someone—when he contacted her about a biography of Mike. But I did. I told him everything about Mike and me because I wanted people to know he loved *me*. Tomorrow morning everyone in New Zealand will read that Aline gave Mike nothing, and I gave him everything.'

Locked in a savage agony of rejection and betrayal, Aline closed her eyes, listening to the meaningless words buzz around inside her head. She craved numbness, forgetfulness, with the avid hunger of an addict.

'And that book's coming out tomorrow?' Jake demanded so silkily that Aline's lashes flew up.

No emotion showed in his face, but his gaze focused on Lauren with the searing lance of a laser. Behind the hard, handsome features Aline saw a predator, menacing, relentless, and lethally dangerous.

Visibly bracing herself, Lauren took an instinctive step backwards. 'It's being launched next week, but tomorrow there'll be a big extract in one of the Sunday papers.' From somewhere she produced an aggressive tone. 'Mike put

New Zealand on the map with his single-handed sailing voyages around the world, and he cared enough about kids to set up the Connor Trust and raise millions of dollars for it. Some of the money from the book's going to the Trust, yet Aline would have stopped publication if she'd been able to.' She cast a scathing glance at Aline. 'People need to know what a wonderful man—a truly great man—he was. I'm not ashamed of loving him, and I'll be proud until I die that he loved me.'

Jake would have liked very much to wrap his hands around that slender throat and throttle the life out of her, but he needed to get Aline out of there before the confrontation—already drawing covert attention—went any further. White and frozen, her subtle cosmetics displayed for the mask they were, she hadn't moved since Lauren had started her attack.

It was the first time he'd seen her at a disadvantage, and he was startled by the fierce protectiveness that unexpectedly gripped him.

Ignoring Lauren, he stepped between the two women and touched Aline's arm. When she didn't respond he said gently, 'Aline, come with me.'

After a taut moment she shivered.

'Let's go,' he said, relieved when she let him steer her out of the nearest door and into the entrance hall, mercifully empty of onlookers.

With a firm hand at her elbow, he led her across the gleaming wooden floor with its priceless Persian rug; he wondered if the door to Keir's study would be locked, but it yielded to his urgent hand.

Mentally thanking Keir for his trust in his guests, he pushed it open, noting with a half-smile that Keir wasn't that trusting; everything but the desk and the bookshelves had been locked away in a bank of cupboards.

Obediently, silently, Aline went ahead, finally stopping in the middle of the room to look around with dazed bewilderment. Succumbing to his concern, Jake folded her slim, cold hands in his, but although she didn't resist it was like touching a statue.

'She could be lying,' he said harshly.

'She's not lying.' Aline's voice sounded distant, muted, empty of the subtle sexy texture that made it so erotic beneath the surface crispness.

'How do you know?'

She shuddered. 'He used to say my eyes were like the very best turquoise. How would she know that unless he told her?'

Pillow-talk, he thought savagely. 'It could have slipped out in conversation.'

She shook her head. 'Keir must know; he was Michael's best friend,' she said. And then with a half-sob, 'Yes, of course. That's why...'

'Tell me,' he commanded when her voice trailed away into nothingness.

She didn't ask him what business it was of his. The shock of Lauren's revelation had smashed the barriers he'd tried so hard to penetrate these past months. Ruthlessly practical, he decided it might be a good thing; if she'd been living in a fool's paradise the truth could only set her free. It might even help the small personal crusade he'd embarked on—finding out exactly what was going on in the Connor Trust.

But, God, he hated to see her in such pain.

In that same empty monotone she said, 'About a year before Michael died I noticed a distance between them, and after that we didn't see much of Keir. I asked Michael why, and he said that it was the natural way of things—married men didn't have so much in common with their single friends.' She lifted her lashes and looked at him with blank eyes like enamelled jewels, their vivid colour framed by long black lashes. 'You believe people when you love them because it hurts too much not to.'

Looking into that lifeless, beautiful face, Jake thought violently that if he could kill a dead man he'd do it right then.

A soft sound from behind alerted him to the opening of the door; instantly he swung around, thrusting Aline behind him as their host entered the room.

Frowning, Keir demanded, 'What's going on here?'

Jake stood to one side and let Aline tell Keir exactly what Lauren had said.

He was good, Jake thought with respect; their host's ice-grey eyes registered only a single flash of fury, but of course Aline noticed.

She whispered, 'Was Lauren the only one?'

'Yes,' Keir said brusquely.

'So he did love her,' she said, as though the words stabbed her to the heart. 'Why didn't you tell me?'

'Would you have believed me?' When she shook her head he added more gently, 'It wasn't my place to tell you.'

Jake understood. He'd been in an impossible position. Was Keir's knowledge the source of the tension he'd sensed between Aline and her boss?

Politely, Aline said, 'Of course it wasn't. I'm sorry I asked. Keir, I think I'd better go now.'

'I'll take you,' Jake told her.

She swivelled as though she'd forgotten he was there. 'That's very kind of you,' she said woodenly, 'but my car's here.'

'You can't drive.' Jake's voice was patient. 'I'll make sure your car gets home.'

He could see her try to muster her defences. 'I'll be perfectly all—'

'You're not fit to drive,' Jake said brutally. 'Kill yourself if you want to, but what if you kill someone else?'

Huge turquoise eyes held his until she made a blundering gesture of rejection, muttering, 'All right, I'll go with you.' She turned back to Keir. 'Please tell Hope I'm sorry?'

'Of course. Will you be all right?' He frowned, his eyes travelling from Aline's shuttered face to Jake's.

With an effort Jake could only imagine, she managed a faint curve of her lips.

'Of course I will. You don't die from disillusion. And I've got this week off—I'll be fine once I've had a chance to get used to the idea of—of...' She choked and caught herself up.

Harshly, Jake said, 'I'll look after her.'

He and Keir exchanged a look, golden eyes clashing with ice-grey. Jake said softly, 'This has nothing to do with you.'

Keir didn't like that, but after several taut seconds he nodded.

Once safely in Jake's car, Aline sat back into the seat and stared at the window, trying desperately to summon a blankness that would blot out her thoughts.

It was useless. All her mind could register was the stark, inescapable fact that Michael had betrayed her.

Eventually she blurted, 'I'm surprised she waited so long to tell me.' The words burst from some secret part of her, rooted in a miserable mixture of anguish and furious humiliation.

'Why would she want to tell you?' Jake asked, backing the car skilfully between two badly parked others.

'For years she hasn't said a word! Why now, I wonder?' And to her astonishment Aline heard herself say, 'I'm so sorry for her; to love someone and not be able to grieve openly for him must be the worst kind of hell. And then to lose her baby...' Her voice trailed off as she remembered that Michael had refused her a child. Stumbling, she said, 'Perhaps she wanted to forewarn me—'

'The baby,' Jake told her with ruthless frankness.

'That's what she saw when she came in the door—you laughing with Emma.'

Aline looked down at her hands, realising they'd taken on a life of their own and were writhing together in her lap in the classic gesture of helpless indecision. Revulsion and sheer force of will subdued them into stillness.

'I see.' She straightened her fingers and stared at the wedding ring she'd worn with such pride ever since Michael had put it on five years previously. It weighed heavy, as crushing as treachery.

Clenching and unclenching her hands, she said thinly, 'I feel a total idiot. Grieving nearly three years for someone who told his lover what pet names he called me!'

'You're not the first person to have your trust betrayed.' Jake's voice was infuriatingly calm, close to off-hand. 'It happens to everyone.'

'To you?' she demanded.

He shrugged. 'Of course.'

Suddenly aflame with reviving anger, she said intensely, 'I'm not going to put myself in such a position again. *Never!*'

Jake glanced across and saw the savage, almost wild determination on her face as she wrenched off the wedding ring and wound down the window. He didn't stop her when she flung the ring through the window. Fresh air whipped around them, carrying the scent of grass and manuka balsam and the faint, salty tang of the sea.

'There,' she said intensely. 'It's over. All I want to do now is forget.'

Brows slightly raised, Jake drove on.

A few miles down the road she said, 'Turn right at the next turn-off. I live—'

'I know where you live—in a townhouse beside the harbour on Whangaparaoa Peninsula,' he told her curtly.

Later she might wonder how he knew her address, but at the moment she couldn't summon up the energy.

But he wouldn't let her sink into the stupor she craved. Coolly persistent, he asked, 'What are your plans?'

'I don't know,' she said dully. She looked around as though in an unknown landscape. 'Stay at home, I suppose. Regroup...'

'Did you live there with him?'

'Who? Oh, Michael. Yes.' Stupid—she'd been so *stupid*! 'I don't want to go back there,' she admitted with painful honesty.

'You could come with me,' he suggested casually. 'I own a beach house not too far away—it's completely isolated. I'm going there tonight for a few days before I leave New Zealand. You can come if you want to.'

She made a jerky movement, then clamped her hands together in her lap. 'I couldn't impose,' she said in her stiffest tone.

His laughter was low and cynical. 'You mean, you think I might try to seduce you. Naturally, after you've had such a huge shock, that's exactly what I'd do. You don't have much of an opinion of me, but, for the record, you won't have to sleep with me.'

Scarlet-faced, she muttered, 'I'm sorry. I didn't mean that.'

Her head drooped sideways. Racked by an exhaustion of the spirit, by waves of tiredness that slowed her brain and made her unable to think sensibly, she muttered, 'I'll be fine. It was kind of you to offer, though. Thank you.'

But when the car drew to a halt outside her house a pleasant and determined young woman, with cameraman and sound recorder in tow, was waiting for her in the street. One or two neighbours were already outside, watching.

Strong face angry, Jake swore beneath his breath. 'Do you want to turn around and get out of here?'

'Where would I go?' she asked, her voice so thin and

apprehensive it horrified her. She dragged in a breath and said between her teeth, 'No, I will *not* run away.'

'Good,' he responded smoothly, pulling in behind the television company van. 'Give them that arrogant stare and walk right over the top of them. Wait in the car until I let you out, and from then on I'll be just behind you.'

Clinging to that promise, Aline straightened her shoulders and disciplined her face as she got out of the car.

'Mrs Connor?' the journalist asked after a rapid, appreciative glance at Jake. 'I wonder if I could have a word with you—?'

'No, thank you,' Aline said, appalled by the cold reptilian scud of fear down her spine. She saw the camera focus and had to hide an impulse to scuttle inside to safety.

'It won't take a moment—it's about Stuart Freely's biography of your husband.' The woman gave a persuasive smile. 'We thought you might like to make some comments.'

'You heard Ms Connor,' Jake said briefly. 'She doesn't want to comment.'

Smirched and sickened by the determined interest she saw in the woman's face, Aline unlocked the door and walked inside.

'It must be a quiet weekend for news,' she said bitterly as Jake closed the door behind him.

'Change your mind and come with me. The uproar will die down in a week or so—the media will soon find something else to feed on.'

'You're very kind,' she said, fear mingling with a restless longing, 'but it would be cowardly—'

'Cowardly? To stop them putting you in a pillory to entertain an audience?' Each scornful word cut through the armour of aloofness she'd erected. 'Come up with a better excuse than that, Aline.'

Aline looked around the sitting room she and Michael had furnished with so much care, so much pleasure. Black

anger and despair gripped her. The thought of spending
one more moment in this shrine to a lie was beyond bear-
ing.

At least in Jake's abrasive company she wouldn't wal-
low in self-pity, imagining Michael and Lauren in each
other's arms, hearing him whisper his love to another
woman...

'All right, I'll come,' she said, weakly surrendering.

'Get some clothes,' Jake commanded. He took a mobile
phone from his pocket and began to punch in numbers.
She watched as he held it to his mouth, his keen raptor's
eyes fixed on her. 'Sally?' he said. 'I've got a couple of
jobs for you, both urgent—'

Aline ran up the stairs and flung clothes from her wardrobe into a weekend bag. Feverishly but automatically, she
stuffed cosmetics and toiletries on top, grabbed a pair of
shoes, and changed from her silk suit into black trousers
and a polo-necked T-shirt the same colour. After pushing
the long sleeves up to her elbows, she slung a black linen
shirt around her shoulders in case it got cold on the boat.

Abruptly her energy drained away; she stood for a long
moment, staring blankly around. Michael smiled at her
from the dressing table. Eyes filling with tears at the loss
of a lovely dream, she walked over and put the photograph
face down in the drawer. One day perhaps she would accept that to have loved him was worth it; all she could feel
now was outrage and humiliation—and an angry, unexpected sympathy for Lauren, because Michael had betrayed them both.

'Have you finished up there?'

'Yes,' she said promptly, and came out of the room.
Behind her, jerked by her ungentle hand, the door closed
with a small crash.

Six foot three of virile, compelling male, Jake waited at
the foot of the stairs, the autocratic angles of his bronze
profile gilded by the late-afternoon sun. Tawny lights glim-

mered in his black hair and a cynical smile hardened his mouth.

He was the ultimate challenge, she thought, stabbed by an urgent, primitive response—a challenge she wasn't up to.

'Do you need help with that bag?' he asked briskly.

Heat burned along her cheekbones. 'No, thank you,' she said, lifting it and walking down the stairs. Instinct warned her that by going with Jake she was setting out on an unknown journey into perilous seas, a journey with no map and no compass. And she was a very weary wayfarer.

Perhaps her mental and emotional exhaustion showed in her face, for Jake took the bag from her and asked in a different voice, 'Do you have a back door?'

'Through there.' She indicated the direction. 'It leads into the garage, and then into an access alley.'

'Good.' His smile twisted as he glanced at her. 'I don't think I've ever seen you when you haven't been dressed in perfect taste. Those are ideal clothes for a fast getaway. Can you walk half a kilometre or so up to the golf course?'

'Of course I can—but why?'

'Because that's where the helicopter will be.'

'The helicopter?' Her voice sounded flat, without inflection, but she didn't care; she struggled to reach that shroud of grey nothingness that shielded her from pain and shock. She'd come to know it well after Michael's death, but it was no longer there for her and she knew why; Jake's raw masculinity had blown it into wispy shreds, leaving her quivering and exposed.

Patiently he said, 'The chopper was to have picked me up in Auckland, but it's on its way here now.'

'What about your car?'

'Someone will drive it back to town,' he told her.

Because it seemed reasonable, Aline nodded and followed him through the back door, docilely handed him the keys and waited while he locked up behind them.

'I'll go ahead,' he said.

But nobody ambushed them in the alley behind the townhouses.

'Most people never think to check the back,' Jake said, locking the gate behind Aline and pocketing the keys. 'Let's get out of here.'

Sometimes, she thought, donning sunglasses as they strode away from the house she'd shared with Michael, it was easier and simpler to give in to an irresistible force. And if that was just another way to say she was a coward—well, so be it.

They had almost reached the golf course when they heard the helicopter coming across the ocean, descending rapidly.

'Walk faster,' Jake said calmly as the *whump-whump-whump* of its engine began to echo. 'No, don't run—we don't want to attract any attention.'

But no one took any notice; people living around this superb golf course were accustomed to the arrival and departure of helicopters. The street was still empty when they turned into the gate and headed for the concrete pad where the chopper was settling with cumbersome accuracy.

The pilot lifted a hand. The door slid open and another man leapt down, crouching as he ran towards them. Jake dropped something into his palm, then grabbed Aline's hand.

'Keep your head down,' he commanded, and towed her up to the open door.

The blast of turbulent air whipped long strands of black hair from the neat coil at the back of her head, tossing it around her cold face. Jake dumped the cases, and in spite of her protests lifted Aline into the machine.

The way her eager flesh reacted to his impersonal grip finally robbed her of any chance of reaching that barren, emotionless refuge she longed for. She might have been able to put the swimming in her head down to the thud of

the rotors, but what set her heartbeat pummelling her
breastbone was Jake's touch, the faint salty fragrance of
his skin, and his effortless strength.

She pushed the tangled locks from her face with shaking
fingers.

By then in the front, Jake turned. 'Seatbelt,' he mouthed,
pointing to the belt with one imperative hand.

Biting her lip, she nodded and groped for the straps.
After watching until she'd buckled them across her waist,
Jake pushed the door closed before reaching for a pair of
headphones. Beneath the fine material of his shirt his body
flexed with spare masculine grace.

Aline watched his lips move as he said something to the
pilot. Was she being incredibly stupid to go with him?

Well, if she was, who cared? She closed her eyes.
Michael, she thought drearily, oh, Michael...

Yet deep in her innermost heart she'd always known
she wasn't enough of a woman to keep Michael satisfied.
Lauren's ripe femininity was what men wanted.

A howling increase in the blast of the engines was followed by a sudden lurch and then lift-off. Aline settled
back and let her eyelids drift up. With bent head, Jake was
checking something in his lap. The westering sun painted
a wash of gold over his face, emphasising its bold stamp
of authority, its stark, forceful command.

Heat seared through her, smashing past the layers of
weary grief. She shivered with muted apprehension as they
flew away from the sunset over water the colour of wine,
heading over peninsulas and bays and islands. How on
earth had she let herself be hijacked like this?

Cowardice, she decided, and Jake's uncompromising
will. She should have seen it coming; she'd soon learned
to respect his intelligence and his grasp of business. He'd
known exactly what he wanted from his association with
the bank, and he'd used his clout and a certain amount of

ruthless power in negotiation, although the final deal satisfied both partners.

Yet beneath the civilised—if aggressive—businessman, she thought with an odd primitive thrill, lurked a warrior, a man with hunting instincts as keenly honed as those marauders who'd swept periodically out of the desert or the forest, or from frozen wastes to plunder and loot and enslave. In spite of his mask of civilised discipline, Jake Howard radiated a primal intensity that slashed through her misery and humiliation, homing in on the basic need of a woman for a man.

When he caught her watching him the arrogantly handsome face didn't change expression, but his unreadable eyes narrowed when he mouthed, 'OK?'

Bitterly angry at the betraying tug of sensation deep in the pit of her stomach, she nodded and glanced away. How odd that she should be torn between grief at the shattering of her memories and this heated awareness of another man.

From their first meeting she'd reluctantly responded to Jake's sexual energy, the supercharged physicality that his expensive tailoring didn't hide, but she'd done her best to ignore it, seeing her unwilling response as treachery to the memory of the man she'd loved with all her heart.

And if that thought didn't hurt so much she'd be laughing at her own naïve foolishness.

Once more she closed her eyes and tried to sink into nothingness. It didn't work.

Angry and tense because Jake's presence kept jerking her back into the real world, she peered sideways, picking out places she recognised—various islands and the intertwined arms of sea and land. The helicopter rode through a sunlit canopy while darkness overtook the land, and in its wake sprang scatterings of golden pinpricks. Trying to keep her mind from fixing obsessively on the man in front, Aline named every cluster and string of lights.

At last it was too dark to see, and she closed her eyes again, only opening them when the helicopter banked.

They landed in a purple and indigo night that bloomed with stars. Jake pushed the door back and swung long legs down; turning, he beckoned Aline.

She fumbled with the seatbelt; once free she hunched her shoulders and eased herself across to the door. Jake didn't move, and when she looked into his face he gave a sudden humourless smile and lifted her down. Frustrated by her involuntary response she stiffened, knocking her temple against the side of the opening.

It hurt, and she said, 'Ouch,' putting up a hand to the slight contusion as he carried her easily across the grass, setting her down well away from the helicopter.

'What happened?' he demanded, running his fingers through her hair to discover the small bump. Frowning, he traced its contours gently.

Shaken by his nearness and his unexpected gentleness, Aline stepped back and shook her head.

'Stay there,' he commanded, and strode back to collect two bags, hers and one that must have been waiting for him on the chopper.

'Thank you,' she said bleakly when he dumped them at her feet.

She picked them up and turned towards the dark bulk of a house. After two or three steps she realised he wasn't with her. A swift glance over her shoulder revealed him unloading a couple of cartons from the helicopter.

Food, of course; he'd have organised it while she'd packed. No, he'd planned this holiday before he'd gone to Emma's christening, so supplies would already have been seen to.

She dropped the bags and started to go back to help unload, but Jake, his rangy body outlined in light from the helicopter, had almost reached her. As he put the cartons down the helicopter rose like a squat, noisy beetle, its lights blinking steadily while it banked above them and then soared away.

Jake straightened up. 'How's your head?' he asked abruptly. 'No headache?'

'No, it was just a small bump.' She cleared her throat. 'It's fine.'

'Welcome to my bach,' he said, and took her hand.

Automatically Aline pulled back, but the warm, strong fingers didn't release her. 'The grass is uneven,' he explained, scooping up the bags and urging her towards the house.

'What about the cartons—?'

'I'll come back for them. Come on, you're cold.'

'I'm not.'

He brought her hand up to his face, pressing it for one tense second against heated skin and the subtle abrasion of his beard. That fleeting contact seared through every quickening cell in her body.

'Definitely cold,' he said calmly. 'Let's get inside.'

And because she didn't want to get involved in an undignified tug of war she couldn't win—*not* because his clasp was strangely comforting—she let her fingers lie in the warmth of his and walked beside him towards the house.

Behind them the chop-chop-chop of motors faded into silence. Stars pulsated above, far brighter than they ever were in the city. A cool breeze flirted across her face, heavy with the delicious perfume of mown grass. Every sense suddenly and painfully alert, Aline pretended to gaze around.

At the house Jake dropped her hand and unlocked a wide door. Pushing it open, he switched on a light inside the door and glanced down at her, his face oddly rigid in the bright flood of light. 'Come in, Aline,' he said with unusual formality.

'I wouldn't call this a bach,' she remarked, hesitating a

cowardly second before bracing her shoulders and walking inside. 'It's far too big and modern. How many bedrooms does it have?'

'Four. I didn't know that baches had to have a certain number of rooms to deserve the name.' His voice was cool, entirely lacking in any undercurrents, but his eyes scrutinised her face with a perceptiveness that screamed an alarm inside her. 'It's built to be easy to look after, suitable for casual holidays, so as far as I'm concerned it's a bach.'

'It's lovely,' she said quickly, looking around with assumed interest.

Apprehension prickled through her. Jake had seen her desperate and hurting; would he use that pain and desperation against her?

Not that it mattered; later her pride might suffer, but for the moment she didn't—wouldn't—let herself care.

She just wished it had been any other man than Jake Howard who'd offered her a refuge.

Perhaps he felt some guilt for that scene with Lauren, but a sideways glance as he strode beside her along the wide, tiled hall dispelled that idea. Why should he? It hadn't been his fault, and anyway, Jake didn't look the sort of man who did guilt.

'Let me see that bump.'

'It's perfectly all right,' she said, voice sharpening. 'I can't even feel it now, and it didn't break the skin.'

But he insisted on parting her black hair with exquisite care so that he could check it. Aline closed her eyes, only to open them swiftly when she found that darkness emphasised his faint male scent—salty and sensual—and the slow fire of his touch on her head. Tensely she bit her lip.

He released her, saying abruptly, 'It's going down already. You're rocking on your feet. I'll show you to your room and you can rest there if you like.'

'I'm fine,' she said. 'It was barely a bump.'

The room he showed her was huge; Aline stood staring

at the vast bed as Jake opened windows, letting in a great swathe of fresh, salty air. 'The bathroom's through that door,' he said, indicating one in the wall. 'I'll bring you something to drink.'

'I don't want—'

'Aline,' he said very softly, his face hard and watchful, 'just let go, will you? You've been running on adrenalin and will-power ever since that bloody woman spilled her guts. A drink will ease a bit of that tension, and a decent meal will give you something to use for energy. At the moment you look like the princess in the tower—white and drawn and so tightly wound you'll shatter if a mosquito lands on you.'

Her chin lifted. 'I don't need a drink to ease tension. I'm not in the habit of "spilling my guts"—' her voice infused his phrase with delicate scorn '—to perfect strangers, thank you.'

He gave her a thin, unsparing smile. 'That sounds more like the Aline Connor I know. Not even my mother said I was perfect, but as for being strangers—I don't think so...'

Something mesmerising in his fierce eyes, in the deep voice, tightened around Aline and imprisoned her in a cage of indecision. Breath clogged her lungs; she heard the distant drumbeat of her pulse, slow and heavy and then faster, faster, as Jake took her face in his hands and tilted it to meet his uncompromising gaze. Two lean forefingers traced the black, winged length of her brows.

Eyes glittering with a crazy mixture of anger and hunger, Aline jerked her head back. 'Let me go,' she said, the words hoarse and laboured.

'We're not strangers, Aline,' Jake said, laughing in his throat as he dropped his hands and stepped a pace away from her. 'Far from it.'

Sickened by the shivering pleasure his expert touch had given her, she said crudely, 'You said I wouldn't have to sleep with you.'

'And I meant it.' He didn't seem angry, although his eyes were calculating. 'But I'm not going to let you lie to yourself. You know as well as I do that from the moment we met we've been acutely, uncomfortably and inconveniently conscious of each other. Sooner or later we're going to do something about it.'

'I won't—'

'Calm down.' He said it so forcefully the words dried on her tongue. 'I've already told you I'm not such an insensitive clod that I'd try to persuade you now. Come out when you're ready.'

Aline waited until the door closed silently behind him before unpacking with rapid, angry energy, stacking her clothes in the walk-in wardrobe next to the bathroom.

Then she gazed around the room—large and light, furnished with a casual expertise that breathed skill and money—and found herself liking it very much.

Retreating, she showered, sighing when her tense muscles finally relaxed under the hot water. But by the time she'd towelled herself dry and dressed—the same black trousers topped this time by a soft silk shirt in the moody aquamarines and blues that went so well with her eyes—she was once more as tight as a coiled spring.

'Stupid!' she muttered between her teeth, picking up the hairdrier. 'So, why wouldn't the bathroom have everything a woman might need? Do you care?'

A twist of jealousy gave her an answer she didn't like. Refusing to consider the highly suspect implications, she used the drier and her brush to free her hair of tangles before winding it firmly into its knot and venturing out of the sanctuary of her room.

'Ah, back to normal,' Jake said enigmatically, looking across the high bar that separated the kitchen from a huge living and dining area. 'A pity—I liked that wild, uncaged look.'

She frowned, shocked anew by the pulse of response

through her. He'd changed too, his long legs and narrow hips shaped by casual trousers, with a tawny, superbly cut cotton shirt clinging to his wide shoulders. Rolled sleeves revealed tanned forearms, and damp hair fell across his brow as he stirred something that smelt delicious.

'The wild uncaged look doesn't fit into corporate life,' she said evenly. 'Can I help?'

'Can you cook?'

'I can stir,' she retorted, irritated at the defensive undertone to the words.

He laughed. 'It's all right—I've got dinner organised.' He set the spoon down and put a lid on the saucepan, then emerged through the doorway and strode across to a sideboard where a tray held a bottle of champagne and two tall flutes.

Aline shuddered. After this afternoon she didn't think she'd ever be able to drink champagne again without recalling Lauren. She said tautly, 'A man who can cook—wonderful!'

'All the great chefs are men,' he said, still amused.

'Not any longer they're not.'

Smiling, he eased the cork from the bottle. His charismatic mixture of confidence and grace and authority made everything he did seem easy.

Aline glanced at the bottle; this wasn't merely champagne, it was superb French champagne. 'Are you trying to *impress* me?' she asked, a cynical smile touching her mouth.

Gleaming gold eyes scanned her face with cool interest. 'Could I?'

CHAPTER THREE

A HEATED recklessness gripped Aline. Tomorrow she'd regret this, but she replied, 'No, you're not trying to impress; that armour-plated confidence is tough enough for you to ignore what anyone thinks.'

Especially a woman he'd seen comprehensively humiliated. Jake probably felt sorry for her, she thought, outraged pride gouging more holes in her disintegrating armour.

'I do have some respect for some people's opinions,' he said dryly.

'But none for public opinion.'

'A hundred and fifty years ago public opinion held that women were unfit to vote.' His smile was ironic. 'Most women believed that too. So, no, I don't listen to public opinion.'

He had the sort of mind that stimulated her, made her want to sharpen her own wits against his. Stubbornly she kept silent as he poured the pale gold liquid into the flutes—lean, tanned hands, strong and deft, capable and expert...

'We should drink a toast,' Jake said. When she looked up sharply he handed her a glass with an enigmatic smile. 'To the truth.'

Aline's mouth twisted. '"And the truth shall make you free"?' she scoffed before she drank. Bitterness spiked her words as she set the glass down onto the polished wood table with an audible click. 'I don't think so.'

'Would you rather still be chained by comfortable lies?' Jake asked sardonically. 'You surprise me.'

Her eyelashes quivered but she kept staring into the

glass. Tiny bubbles beaded and winked, rising in columns to the surface of the champagne. 'Why?'

'Surely you'd rather deal with a painful truth than live a lie.' He waited, and when she said nothing he added deliberately, 'You've always struck me as being as strong and fine as spun steel. Only weaklings hide behind convenient falsehoods.'

Aline lifted the glass to her lips again. Although some detached part of her brain conveyed to her that the champagne was dry and exquisite, it might have been sour milk for all the pleasure she took in it. 'I'm gratified you think I'm strong,' she said, folding her lips on the other words that threatened to tumble out and angry with herself for saying that much. Vulnerability brought predators prowling.

Sure enough, Jake's glance sharpened. 'But?'

She summoned a light, casual shrug and a cool smile. 'Sometimes it's the only thing a person's got going for them, and steel is utilitarian stuff.'

His brows met over the blade of his nose. 'The world runs on utilitarian stuff,' he said dispassionately, watching her with unsettling curiosity. 'Steel, coal, oil, trees felled to make paper, metals dug from the ground, food grown in the earth. Are you a closet romantic, Aline, yearning for moonbeams?'

'No,' she said with a brittle lack of emphasis, tight shoulders moving uneasily under his intent golden scrutiny. She thought to sip some more champagne, but put the glass down untouched. The last thing she needed was a head clouded by bubbles.

The glimmer of starlight on the sea gave her an opportunity; she walked across to uncurtained windows and gazed out. 'What a lovely spot you have here.'

It was a clumsily obvious ploy, but to her relief he let her get away with it. Ten minutes later they were discussing a controversial takeover that had been exercising the minds of financial journalists for the past week.

Usually Aline could do this sort of thing without thinking, but tonight Jake's trenchant, perceptive comments kept prodding her brain out of neutral; by the time dinner was ready she realised with sick shame that she hadn't thought of Michael for at least an hour.

At first she ate the scallop and noodle salad automatically, hardly tasting the sophisticated lime juice and sesame oil dressing, but soon the bite of chilli and fresh ginger and the smooth richness of the scallops shook her tastebuds awake.

'That was delicious,' she said with real appreciation when she'd finished. 'You're not just a man who can cook—you're a superb cook.'

'Thank you,' he said laconically.

Aline watched as he collected the plates and took them into the kitchen. The combination of food and champagne and impersonal yet exhilarating conversation, the strange novelty of being cosseted and cared for, both stimulated and lulled her into a languid mood.

Jake was dangerous. When all she'd wanted to do was hide for the rest of her life he'd forced her senses and mind into enjoyable alertness. Simply by being himself—a compelling, attractive man—he'd broken through the bitterness of betrayal.

Heat surged from deep inside her, stinging her skin, clouding reason and logic in fumes of sensation. Shakily she got up and walked across the big room, pushing back the folding doors to gulp in cool air, moist from the sea, lush with the scent of greenery. She didn't want to feel, to cope, to recover; for once in her life she longed to hide and howl at her emptiness.

When Jake came in from the kitchen carrying a couple of serving dishes she asked with tight formality, 'Do you mind if I leave the doors open?'

'No,' he said, setting the dishes down. He straightened and stood watching her as she came towards her.

Something about his stillness, the metallic light in his golden eyes, the controlled lines of his sculpted mouth, chased ripples of unease across Aline's skin. Lightly, steadily she said, 'I was suspiciously close to nodding off, and I don't want to miss any of this superb dinner.'

His smile was enigmatic. 'Then sit down and eat it.'

An hour later she sighed, 'No, no coffee, thank you. That was a wonderful feast. Where on earth did you learn to cook—or were you a chef in a previous incarnation?'

'I couldn't afford to eat out when I was at university,' he said, getting up and holding out his hand to her. 'So I learnt how to make a decent meal. I like to be good at what I do.'

Oh, she believed him. At everything he did, she thought, trying to banish an image of him making love, bronzed skin gleaming...

'Who taught you?' She let her hand lie in his, adding with a brittle smile, 'The current girlfriend, I suppose.'

'A restaurant.'

He let her go, but before she had time to feel bereft he supported her elbow in an easy grip, startlingly warm through the fine silk of her sleeve.

Shamed by the untamed frisson of need zigzagging through her, she said, 'A restaurant altruistic enough to give lessons in gourmet cooking to penniless university students? If only I'd known about it I might be able to cook something more sophisticated than scrambled eggs.'

'If you can make a good fist of those you can cook anything,' he said, steering her towards the seating area. 'I started in the kitchen as a part-time hand and gradually rose through the ranks. By the time I finished my degree I was allowed to cook the odd dish if the chef was in a good mood and there weren't too many customers that night.'

Something—probably the second glass of champagne she'd been unwise enough to drink—persuaded her to confess, 'I can produce very basic meals, but that's all.'

'Yes,' he said austerely, 'you look as though you survive on salads. Don't you enjoy cooking?'

She shrugged, collapsing into a sofa that faced the wide open doors. 'My sister was the domestic daughter. She could conjure a fantastic meal from some stale cheese, a couple of lettuce leaves and a spoonful of chutney, so she went to gourmet cooking classes while I collected degrees. I was going to follow my father into his business.'

He switched off the lights.

'What are you doing?' she demanded, jerking bolt upright.

'Any moment now you'll see the moon rise over the Coromandel Peninsula. It's worth watching.' His amused tone further unsettled her.

However, when she heard the soft sounds of him settling into a chair close by she relaxed her taut body, turning her head to look at the little bay. Miles away, over a waste of sea that trembled in the starshine, a faint glow outlined a high hill.

Out of the darkness Jake asked casually, 'So did you follow your father into the business?'

'No.'

Silence stretched between them until he prompted, 'What happened?'

'My sister and mother were killed in a car accident.' Aline looked down at her lap and carefully untangled her knotted fingers. 'My father sold the business and used the money to set up a foundation in their memory.' She paused, before finishing evenly, 'And then he killed himself.'

Because she kept her eyes fixed onto the scene outside, she neither heard Jake move nor saw him. As moonlight rimmed the horizon in silver she felt the sofa cushions give beside her. Her skin burned with primitive awareness and she had to concentrate on her breathing.

'A cruel and cowardly thing to do.' His voice was corrosively contemptuous.

'It's all right,' she said calmly, holding herself upright to fight an abject weakness that craved the warmth and the solid support of his powerful body. 'I understood. He loved them very much.'

Jake's silence had a forbidding undercurrent. She finished, 'It was almost six years ago; I've got over it.'

'So well that you have to gird yourself up when you speak of it?' he asked coolly. He ran a swift, unsparing hand the length of her spine from her shoulder to her waist. 'Pure steel,' he said thoughtfully. 'Did you cry for them?'

'I'm not a freak! Of course I cried for them.' Aline fought back the spurt of anger to add more temperately, 'But you can't cry for ever. Sooner or later you have to leave the past behind.'

'Something your father was too cowardly to do, apparently.' His scathing tone revealed his lack of sympathy for those who wallowed in grief. Instead of returning to his chair, he leaned back into the cushions.

Aline stole a swift sideways glance as she inched away from him until stopped by the arm of the sofa. The moon had risen, filling the night with a glowing, coppery radiance that turned in a breath to silver. Against the light Jake's profile outlined power and force, controlled yet dangerous.

He said, 'Tell me about your husband. What made him set up that trust?'

Even as he said the words he wondered savagely what the hell he thought he was doing. She'd had too many betrayals in her life and here he was contemplating the possibility of another.

Night-attuned eyes scanned the pale oval of her face, turned resolutely to the rising moon. With her shoulders squared at right angles to a wand-straight spine, her tilted chin, Aline's whole body expressed a slender, indomitable refusal to surrender. He felt her resentment, knew that the large turquoise eyes would be flat and opaque.

That inconvenient protectiveness—more debilitating than the restless lust that stirred his groin—almost made him give up, but he'd made a promise.

Expecting a flat refusal, a curt suggestion to mind his own business, he was surprised when she answered. 'Hope Carmichael reminds me a bit of Michael—partly it's the colouring, so warm, as though the sun's always shining on them. My sister and mother were like that too—they attracted people like magnets and wherever they went they brought laughter and empathy with them like gifts.'

Jake watched her unblinkingly. Buried deep beneath the cool, level tone was a resigned envy, as though her own talents were worth nothing; her father's legacy, probably.

Jake found himself thoroughly disliking the man who'd convinced her she wasn't worth staying alive for.

He enjoyed women, but none had intrigued him like Aline, hiding her passionate intensity beneath a guarded self-possession. He wanted that caged passion for himself.

Now, however, was not the time. Ruthlessly tamping down his familiar hunger, he observed, 'And Michael Connor?' She stayed stubbornly silent, so he remarked, 'As well as a superb yachtsman, he was a brilliant photographer. I've seen his *Oceans* collection.'

In that still, distant voice she said, 'Yes. He loved the sea.'

'How did he die?' He knew, of course; the man had been a bloody hero.

He heard the swift indrawn breath but her voice was steady. 'He was out with Search and Rescue looking for a friend in the Southern Ocean. He went down in a helicopter. They never found his body.'

Jake said roughly, 'Hell for you.'

'Yes,' she whispered. 'And now it seems I never had his heart either.'

At last she slumped. Jake caught her, pulling her against him in a futile attempt to keep her demons at bay with his strength and his heat. Her slender, fragrant body shook, and he wondered if she was crying.

She said steadily, 'He set up the Trust because he'd had a mentor, a high school teacher, who gave him faith in himself and the courage to strive for what he wanted. He used to say that if it hadn't been for that man he'd have ended up on the streets. He wanted to give something back.'

No tears in her voice, in her words; she hadn't cracked yet. Reluctantly Jake admired her sheer guts, although holding her was playing hell with his control. To take his mind off his damned awkward physical response, he said, 'So he organised an appeal and New Zealanders subscribed by the millions.' Literally. 'Do you have anything to do with it?'

After a pause so short he'd not have noticed if it had been anyone else, she said, 'No.'

She was lying. Jake said nothing, sardonically counting it a triumph when she stayed in his arms as the moon leapt from behind the hills, blotting out the stars with its glory. It brooked no rivals, the moon; Jake wondered whether Michael Connor had been like that.

Well, he enjoyed a challenge. That Aline might have the answer to the riddle he was trying to unravel made things more complicated, but in the end he'd have the answer—and he'd have her too.

The night blinded Aline with its beauty. 'Moonlight is such a familiar miracle,' she said, listening to his heartbeat, stable and strong against her cheek. She realised that it was picking up speed, and something inside her cracked and dissolved and was swept away. In spite of every warning female instinct handed down through the generations, she wanted to trust Jake.

'Entirely familiar, and yet never the same. Like love,' he said deliberately.

Soon she'd pull away. 'Have you ever been in love?'

'I've thought I was occasionally.'

'I've only thought it once,' she said on a note of bitterness. 'I've been waiting for him to come back for almost three years.' She was silent again, and then she said, 'I wonder if he ever loved me.'

'Probably.'

She thought of Lauren. 'Not enough,' she said soberly.

'Men can separate love from sex.' Jake's voice was smooth.

'Would you do that? Make love to a woman when you'd promised to love and stay faithful to another?'

She felt his chest lift, and when he spoke she heard wry resignation in his tone. 'No.'

A simple word, easy to fake, but she believed him. Business was different from personal relationships, yet in business dealings the true nature of a man came through. Jake was tough, a hard negotiator, an astute, formidable businessman with an ice-cold intelligence she'd learned to admire and respect. And he was honest.

'Nor would Keir,' she said quietly. 'He loves Hope so much I can't believe he'd ever be unfaithful. Perhaps I just chose the wrong man.' She gave a half-laugh. 'Except that he chose me. And I think he must have loved Lauren—he told me we should wait to start a family.'

'You could have been looking for something he wasn't able to give,' Jake said.

'Like what?'

'Commitment?'

Only the fine material of Jake's shirt beneath her cheek shielded her from the heat of his body. He smelt of himself—faint, clean and somehow safe. She drifted for long moments, oddly secure, and then said, 'I wasn't enough for him.'

'Enough what?' he asked cuttingly.

She shrugged, finding it strangely easy to talk to him in this dark room with the moon in glory outside, its light path rippling across the miles of sea in front of them. 'Enough woman, I suppose.'

He pulled her around, half lifting her across his legs so that she faced him. In the dim room his features were darkly imperious and angry. 'You are more woman than most men ever dream of,' he said forcefully. 'You're a woman who takes up residence in a man's mind, tremendously sophisticated, composed and discriminating, a challenge that won't go away, won't leave a man alone.'

'And all that means nothing compared to women who are bright and warm and sexy—women like Hope. Or Lauren.' She made to swing her legs down. 'You don't know anything about me, Jake.'

'I know one thing,' he said in a low, dangerous voice, tipping her chin up with a ruthless hand. For a taut moment he stared into her pale face, then said between his teeth, 'I know that if I don't kiss you now I'm going to regret it. And if I do I'll probably regret it even more. But, hell, taking risks is part of living.'

She couldn't move, waiting for the unknown—longing for it. Gently, purposefully, his mouth traced the upward sweep of her brows, her cheekbones, the length of her throat.

And even when he kissed her lips it was almost carefully, until something exploded between them with all the temptation of original sin.

Aline had kissed in love, kissed in affection and commiseration. She had never kissed like this before, wildly, with incendiary ardour, losing every sensible thought the second his mouth took hers and then drowning in the sensation of his expert kisses, ablaze with it, shaking with the energy it summoned—languorous and powerful and fever-ish.

In the end all she could do was surrender.

When Jake lifted his head she opened her eyes, shivering at the stark, stripped hunger in his face.

She'd loved Michael yet he'd never done this to her. Jake Howard, with his warrior's face and warlock's ability to ravish her senses, had worked some black magic and set a dangerous desire thrumming through her veins, a desire so strong she could forget everything by yielding to it.

'I've wanted to do that ever since we met,' she said raggedly, no longer worried about protecting herself.

'Did it satisfy you?' he asked thickly.

She shook her head. 'I want you to make love to me.'

'It doesn't work that way,' he said, but his arms still held her against his lean, aroused body. 'Making love isn't something one person does to another.' Before she could do more than flinch, he went on, 'When we make love, Aline, we'll do it together because that's the only way it has any meaning. But it's not going to happen now, not tonight.'

The flinty note in his voice told her that he wasn't going to change his mind.

Just another rejection.

'Why?' Damn, her voice sounded croaky, as though she was going to cry. She sat up and began to pull away. When he didn't let her go she stopped struggling; she should, she thought, feel physically threatened by his strength and unwavering will.

She didn't.

'You've had a hell of a shock today; you're not fully in control.' His mouth hardened. 'If we made love you'd regret it the moment you woke tomorrow. Probably the moment you climaxed in my arms.'

An exquisite thrill shot down her spine. It gave her the courage to say honestly, 'I don't care.'

He didn't soften. 'I don't want to be used so that you can revenge yourself on a man who's been dead for almost three years.'

'It's not that,' she protested, startled and dismayed.

'Then what is it?' he asked grimly. 'A sudden rush of blood to the head? To be even blunter, if we made love now you'd be using me.'

'But you'd be using me too,' she pointed out, feeling that she'd die if she didn't follow this thing through to the end. 'You want me, and I've wanted you ever since we met. Surely that's all we need?' She shivered.

That sensuous, involuntary shiver smashed right through his confident ability to resist her—that shiver, and her smouldering, avid eyes.

Jake realised that for the first time in his life he was going to ignore his game plan.

It no longer seemed important. Aline—composed, tantalising Aline, with her intelligence and her touch-me-not beauty—had the power to confuse his thinking, heat his blood with an urgent summons as imperative as it was seductive and shatter his will-power into unmourned shards.

Slender as a thoroughbred yet enticingly curved, she smelt of woman: mysterious, infinitely desirable, potent with an age-old enchantment more powerful than mere charm or beauty.

Every sensible caution dissolved in the searing reality of her red mouth as she kissed his throat through the open neck of his shirt. Jake had been about seventeen when he'd last been kissed like that—tentatively, almost shyly—yet behind Aline's kiss sizzled a vibrating intensity that set him alight.

Violent hunger throbbing through him, he looked down at her sleek black head, and did something else he'd

wanted to do for months; he slid his fingers into her knot
of hair and gently levered the strands free, letting them fall
across his wrists like midnight silk, cool and sensuous and
erotic. She didn't even wince, so the bruise had gone.

In a tone too abrasive, too raw, he muttered, 'I don't
want you waking up tomorrow morning and regretting
this.' Deep in his brain he heard an echo of ironic laughter
because he was the one who'd be doing the regretting.

Once again he fought for control, reminding himself
why he shouldn't be doing this, but his resistance faded
when she leaned back and looked him full in the face.
Moonlight lingered lovingly across her features, pooled
along her cheekbones, enlarged her eyes into huge, dark
mysteries.

'I know what I want.' When he went to speak she
clamped a slender, surprisingly strong hand over his
mouth. 'Michael's been dead for almost three years, and
this has nothing to do with him. As you pointed out,
there's been something between us since we first met, and
I want to know what it is.' Her voice deepened in frustration, its intriguing texture intensifying so that it stroked
across him like a summons to paradise. 'I want *you*, Jake.'

God, this was more than flesh and blood could stand!
He closed his eyes, then covered her hand with his, pressing the slender fingers against his mouth so that he could
bite the palm. Her gasp finally splintered his waning resistance.

He opened his eyes to see her staring at him, wide eyes
dilating with a mixture of shock and fever.

Carefully he lifted her hand from his mouth, pushed it
between the buttons of his shirt and settled it on his chest.
Her long fingers flexed and curled against his skin, blasting
pleasure through him.

'Yes,' he said harshly, eyes narrowing.

Aline's pulses jumped at the note in his voice, his
drawn, angular intensity. She thought she might faint with

anticipation as they sat staring at each other, locked into stillness by an impulse that went deeper than the sexuality pulsing between them. Those intense moments were a primitive claiming, she thought, a bonding beyond the physical.

Jake's face was like chiselled stone, only the slight blurring of his mouth showing any softness. I did that when I kissed him, she thought with a fierce pride. His eyes glittered like chips of fire, searching, probing, penetrating.

He said her name on a harsh, darkly possessive intonation.

Feverish shudders raked her skin. Leaning forward, she touched his chin with her mouth, bit along his jaw. When she felt him tense beneath her mouth that inner wildness tightened into an unbearable pleasure.

He stood up, arms coiling around her with supreme, calm strength. 'I know a better place for this,' he said curtly.

Silently he carried her through the darkened room, past the kitchen and into the short passage that led to her bedroom. There he bent his head and kissed her again, a shockingly intimate kiss that coaxed her mouth open.

Erotic, shattering and wonderful, the kiss lasted until he shouldered open the door into her bedroom. Not bothering to close it, Jake walked noiselessly across to the bed. Halfway there, when one of her shoes fell from her foot, Aline barely noticed.

He released her slowly, sliding her down his body until her feet reached a floor that rocked beneath her.

This time she was sure she'd faint. While her tension and arousal were hidden his were blatantly obvious—rampant and arrogantly male, the most primal signal of desire, and her doing.

'It's all right,' he said, hard hands gripping her waist.

Clutching his shoulders, her voice a husky whisper in the room, Aline asked, 'Testing me?'

His laugh was short and unamused. 'Perhaps,' he said enigmatically, lifting his hands from her waist. They slid upwards, coming to rest just beneath her breasts.

Excitement shortened her breath. She pressed herself against him, winding her arms around his broad shoulders and pulling him into her. 'Jake,' she whispered.

His thumbs stroked along her curves, almost delicately in spite of his strength.

Instantly her breasts tightened and became heavy, the nipples beading beneath her bra so acutely sensitive she bit back a cry. She began to undo the buttons of his shirt, taking her time because her hands were shaking.

A flutter of movement over his shoulder whipped her head up.

Instantly Jake swung around, interposing himself between her and the window in one swift, silent movement. Ghosting the words, he asked, 'What is it?'

'Just the curtain in the breeze.'

'Sure?'

'Positive.'

He turned and checked it. 'I can close the windows.'

'No,' she said. 'I want them open.'

He laughed deep in his throat. 'I could take this shirt off for you if you want me to, but I'm enjoying the way you're doing it.'

Deftly Aline went back to work until the garment fell open. 'It's finished,' she said huskily, stroking the skin beneath.

A quick shrug flicked the shirt onto the floor.

'Now I'll do the same for you,' he said, his voice steady with a bold male triumph.

Aline watched as he unfastened the button at her throat, and then moved to those at her breast, his hands bronze against the silk. Spears of hot expectancy pierced her. She fought for breath, wondering how it had happened, this intense anticipation for a man she barely knew.

Well, she'd tried love and it hadn't worked for her, she thought. Now she'd give sex a try.

Yet even as the cynical words formed in her brain she knew that there was more to this than surrender to a physical urge. She might not love Jake, but what she felt for him—this powerful, compelling force—was at least honest.

A cool wash of air warned her that her shirt was hanging free. Jake pushed the soft material back from her shoulders, then stopped. 'That's a pretty chain,' he said neutrally.

Michael had given it to her.

Aline dragged the fragile gold thing over her head and threw it across the room, turning back before it landed. 'It's gone,' she said huskily.

He looked down at her; lit by the moonglow outside, she could see the frown that drew his brows together.

'It's over,' she told him, and when he still didn't move she kissed the swell of muscle in one broad shoulder, kissed it and licked it, and bit into the smooth, heated skin with her sharp teeth. His taste flooded her mouth in a primal signal.

When she heard his jagged indrawn breath and felt his arms close around her with bruising force, for the first time she accepted with a deep, inner confidence that she too possessed sexual power. He asked harshly, 'Are you sure?'

'Very sure,' she said as her shirt slid to the floor.

Jake kissed her, unclipping her bra at the same time with an expertise that shouted his experience.

Her bright, breathless anticipation dimmed—but why? She knew he was no virginal knight of old. Neither was she a maiden pure.

He said in a voice that grated on her ears, 'You are so *beautiful*—perfect for me,' and eased the bra over her shoulders and down her arms.

With it went any pretensions to modesty; at last she

would know what this man offered, and she wanted it so much she didn't care about tomorrow. She whipped off the black scrap of cloth and tossed it in the same general direction as Michael's chain. His betrayal meant nothing now. This was more important.

In a hoarse, uncertain voice she said, 'You're beautiful too.' She shaped his shoulders, fingers pressing into his skin in a slow, tactile exploration. 'And I'm not perfect— I'm just a woman, Jake.'

His hands smoothed from her throat to the first gentle swell of her breasts, sending chills throughout her.

Still in that dark, feral voice, he murmured, 'No, you're not just a woman. Never *just* a woman. You're *more* woman than any man has a right to expect. Or even hope for.'

And he kissed her.

Momentarily she panicked, dimly aware through the erotic fog that clogged her brain that she had to tell him he was wrong—she didn't have what it took to satisfy a man. A warning thundered in the back of her brain, because sex with Jake was going to change everything—for the rest of her life she'd be tied to this memory.

And then he kissed her breast, his mouth discovering the acutely sensitive aureole, and sensation exploded through her, violent, piercing, sweeping every coherent thought before it in a tide of riotous excitement.

He picked her up and deposited her on the bed, looking down at her with gleaming eyes as he stripped off his trousers and then hers. Shocked and disturbed by the intensity of her emotions, Aline stared mutely at him until he came down beside her, big, dominating, a man to die for—a man to fear on some fundamental level.

And then every cowardly fear was banished by the heat of his body, by the skilful, ruthless caress of his hands, his mouth, the slick slide of skin against skin while he taught her more than she had ever known about making love.

Aline learned that each square inch of her skin was available for pleasure, that the pleasure could contract to a single, exquisitely unmerciful point of need until she had to stifle moaned pleas for an unknown satisfaction.

As he kissed her, as he touched her and claimed her, as his mouth took possession of her body, she learned that his scent changed when he made love. One glance lost her in the fiery glitter of his eyes; his expression of hard desire told her that she was returning him the same anguished pleasure he was summoning in her.

But when at last his lean, knowledgeable hand reached the most intimate part of her, seeking yet subtle, she stiffened.

'I won't hurt you,' he soothed, although a rasping thread through each word warned her he was losing the battle for control.

'I know.' But she couldn't stop herself from stiffening again as his fingers slid into her.

Moonlight flooded into the room—silver and darkness, the heat from his body and the cool night air, the scent of the sea and...

'Jake,' she muttered, hungry for something more, arching into him.

'Yes,' he said simply, and rolled her beneath him, entering her with one fierce thrust that linked them—linked them for ever, she thought dazedly as her body stretched to accommodate his, as the heated sensual anticipation transmuted into something wilder, something she could no longer control.

Forcing up heavy eyelids, she saw the harsh contours of his face above her, the black glitter of passion in his eyes, the lips drawn back in a rictus of unbearable pleasure.

She surrendered to it, moving against him, enclosing him, and he thrust even deeper, reaching beyond her body and into her soul, the part of herself she'd always kept separate.

A choked cry strangled in her throat; afire with need, she lifted herself against him in mute pleading, and he gave her what she longed for, at first slowly, as though afraid of hurting her, and then with an increasing, unsparing intensity that tossed her over some precipice and into a firestorm of sensation.

Dimly she heard him groan, felt him drive into her with such ferocity that it tossed her higher into ecstasy if that was possible, and then she fell into freefall, languidly coming down in a softness of after-haze, locked against the heat and power of his body.

Breathing heavily, he turned on his side, a long arm pulling her into him.

'Sleep now,' he said.

Aline's last thought was that now Michael was truly dead to her.

The moon was still sailing serenely high in the sky when she woke. For a moment she froze, but memory flooded back, and she smiled through lips a little tender from Jake's kisses, and stretched a body aching mildly from his slow, skilful, passionate possession.

He was no longer beside her; startled, she sat up. It took only a moment to find him, a dark silhouette out on the terrace, staring across the sea, big and dominant and alone. She'd wanted to coil herself around him, gently woo him into wakefulness, but he had removed himself from that temptation.

Her smile fading into poignant regret, Aline swallowed to ease her dry throat.

No, she didn't want to talk to him now; she felt fragile, disconnected from her real self, on the cusp of the past and the future. She'd drink a glass of water in the bathroom and then she'd pretend to be asleep.

Quietly she got up; warily keeping an eye on that brood-

ing figure in the moonlight, she tiptoed across the room to
the door leading to the walk-in wardrobe and bathroom.

In the bathroom, dimly lit by the lovers' moon, she drew
a glass of water and drank it down. It eased her throat, but
not her sore heart, or her sense of fate in the balance.
You're letting him get to you, she scoffed silently as she
negotiated her way back.

Once in the bedroom she cast a quick glance at the open
windows, frowning when she realised that the deck was
empty. And the bed. Movement down by the water's edge
revealed Jake standing on the sand, still looking away from
her. Her breath locked in her throat. Naked, with the
moon's loving light pouring over his dark head, outlining
every sleek, sculpted muscle, every long, rangy line of his
lithe body, he looked like some primeval god from the
dawn of time, a physical dream of all that was male.

Aline took an involuntary step towards the window. Her
foot hit something and she twisted and fell, thinking, I
should have picked up my shoe! as she landed heavily.
Pain exploded through her head; she lay supine for a few
seconds before it eased back to a dull ache, then crawled
back to the bed, pulling herself into it before sleep
claimed her.

CHAPTER FOUR

THE dream dwindled, evaporating swiftly into bleak nothingness. Engulfed by sorrow and desolation, she buried her face in the pillow in an attempt to reject the day.

It didn't work. After a few moments of formless grief she lifted her head and opened wet, reluctant eyes.

Open curtains allowed sunlight to spill into the room in golden swathes. Big and sparsely furnished in a cool, subtle palette of sand and toffee and cream, the bedroom looked across a lawn onto a curved beach the exact colour of the tiles on the floor.

Narrowing astonished eyes against the final blur of tears, she stared at the sea, restless in the early-morning sunlight that glittered along the waves like a fringe of diamonds.

She had never seen the room before.

Or the beach.

Slowly, cautiously, she turned her head. Just in her line of sight on the tiled floor lay a pair of shoes—low-heeled, black. One stood upright, the other on its side a little distance away, as though the owner had kicked it off.

Or as though it had dropped from a dangling foot...

The warm weight across her shoulders moved. Stunned, she jerked around to meet lazy golden eyes in a hard-hewn, handsome face—a face she didn't know.

Her horrified mind skittered away from the implications as he smiled, a slow, sexy smile that dried her mouth and set her pulse-rate soaring. 'Good morning,' he drawled in a rough early-morning voice.

'Who *are* you?' she blurted, disgusted with herself for sleeping with a man she didn't know.

He froze. Tension danced like a razorblade across the

silence as that purely male smile hardened into something like cruelty. Thick black lashes hid his amazing eyes while he stretched a magnificently naked body with the ease and grace of a large predator. Heat from his skin blasted hers. Pulses thudding, she realised that she too wore no clothes.

The sheet tightened over her bare skin as she jack-knifed away to perch stiffly on the edge of the bed, huddling the sheet around her.

Her unknown lover sat up, revealing broad shoulders and so much tanned skin her blood pressure shot through the roof.

At least she had excellent taste in men, she thought numbly.

Incredibly good-looking, with an angular face that had probably fired a million feverish feminine fantasies, he lounged back against the pillows. 'I don't know whether to be resigned or furious.'

Although no emotion shaded his deep, intriguing voice, she sensed anger simmering beneath the words, and some pointed instinct warned her that this man's anger was not to be taken lightly.

'I don't know what you mean,' she said stupidly, shocked and frightened because her mind was completely empty, as though she'd sprung full-blown to life that morning, in this bed...

His straight black brows rose. In a tone underpinned by mockery, he said, 'It's usually taken as a sign that a man has failed to perform adequately if his lover wakes up crying.' He waited for her to say something, then added on a taunt, 'Not that you seemed to be worrying about anything missing last night.'

Shamed colour burned her skin as he stretched out a muscular arm to touch the drying tearstains at the corners of her eyes, sending a reckless throb of sensation through her.

'So why these?' he asked with cool, sardonic courtesy,

his eyes turning metallic at her helpless flinch. On a flinty note he said, 'Cut out the maidenly embarrassment, Aline. It isn't necessary.'

Aline. Was that her name? It meant nothing.

Panic clawed her and she began to shake as he finished mercilessly, 'You've been married. And last night you were everything you could be—erotic, lusty and more than willing. You made love to me with a far from virginal fervour.'

The faint emphasis on the word 'me' echoed ominously. His words jumping and jangling in her head, she fixed on the most important. 'Married?'

His ruthlessly beautiful mouth twisting, he said, 'If you're conscience-stricken because you've been unfaithful to the saintly Michael, let me remind you he's been dead for almost three years. It's time you let him go.'

She shook her head, searching through her mind for memories of a dead husband and finding only echoing, empty caverns. 'Who *are* you?' she asked again, her words strained and desperate.

Contempt gleamed in his half-closed eyes. 'Stop it now—it's not working,' he said softly, lethally. 'I'm the man you made love with last night, the man whose arms you slept in.'

Unable to meet that probing gaze, she dropped her face into her hands. 'I don't know who you are,' she blurted unevenly, trying to flog her aching brain into producing a memory. When it remained obstinately and terrifyingly empty she wailed, 'I don't even know who *I* am. I don't know where this is. I don't know—I don't know anything!'

In the taut silence the mattress dipped, and in spite of herself she peered from the fragile refuge of her fingers. Her breath stopped in her throat as he strode across the room.

He was huge, she thought frantically. Well over six feet, with shoulders wide enough to hide behind and a lean, poised athlete's body stripped of every ounce of superfluous flesh.

Scratches scored those muscled shoulders, that powerful back. In spite of the blank nothingness in her mind, she knew she'd put them there in an extreme of ecstasy, just as she understood that the mild, sensuous ache in her body was the result of making love, that the taste in her mouth was his, that the scent of the bedclothes was an erotic mingling of male and female.

Appalled, she felt heat gather in her stomach, sing through her in mindless recollection as he disappeared through a door. It seemed that her body had a memory separate from her brain, a physical understanding of their lovemaking, and wasn't shy of showing it—in fact, she realised sickly, it was readying itself for more.

Ashen-faced, she watched as the door opened again and the man who'd made love to her came back in, a dark green bath towel fastened in a knot at his hips. Like a bronzed statue, he was so stunningly perfect as a male, so dangerously disturbing, that Aline's heart almost juddered to a stop.

'I should have realised you'd come up with something like this,' he said, the scorn in his tone shredding her shaky composure even more. When he walked across to the bed she forced her shoulders to remain straight, her chin to tilt at a defiant angle.

'For your information,' he said coldly, his eyes sliding with insulting thoroughness over her face and her bare shoulders, 'I am Jake Howard, and, just in case your mind really was so overwhelmed by last night that it can't function yet, you are Aline Connor.'

Frowning, she tasted both names, turned them over in her mind, her nerves tightening as they summoned nothing. Closing her eyes against the hideous rush of panic, she dropped her head in her hands, shielding her face from his ruthless scrutiny.

'You can stop playing games,' Jake Howard said curtly. 'Last night you made love to me with your eyes and your mouth and your hands, with every subtle movement of that elegant body. Last night, Aline, you knew damned well what you were doing. You asked me to make love to you—'

Humiliated, she clamped her hands over her ears.

Lean fingers prised them away and he continued inflexibly, 'If I didn't satisfy you, then say so; don't hide behind a stupid charade that wouldn't take in a child. It's too late for regrets—you made the decision.'

'I can't remember,' she whispered, trembling in his grasp, her entreating eyes lifted to his. 'I can't remember last night, I can't remember my name or my job, I can't remember anything at all.' Before she had a chance to rein it in, her voice soared perilously high, perilously near to a total loss of control. She swallowed and clamped her mouth tightly over the hysteria that threatened to burst from her. Blinking furiously, she fought to stay calm.

Jake Howard let her wrists go as though they contaminated him and stepped back, his brows meeting above the blade of his nose, the beautiful face stern and uncompromising. 'You must be pretty desperate to try such a banal trick. See if a shower helps.' His tone changed into cool irony. 'Although you might want to forget last night, you know damned well that I took with intense enjoyment everything you offered.'

He waited while colour flamed through her face, and added with brutal assurance, 'And you did offer, Aline. You offered—and you gave—everything I asked for. You enjoyed making love with me. That's what the problem is, isn't it? You gave me more than you wanted to, so to save your pride you're embarking on this shoddy pretence of losing your memory.'

'I'm *not* pretending,' she shouted. 'I don't lie.'

'How do you know that if you've lost your memory?'

She gave him a shocked look, but the gleam in the brilliant eyes sent her glance darting sideways. 'I don't—know,' she whispered, yet was somehow sure that she didn't take refuge in dishonesty.

His wide shoulders lifted in a contemptuous shrug. 'This seems a very selective form of amnesia. I don't know much about it, but I think it's usually caused by physical trauma to the head.'

Before she could stop him he ran long fingers through her hair and over her scalp. He wasn't rough, but she licked her lips nervously, too conscious of the strength in those lean fingers.

And bitterly, terrifyingly conscious too of her involuntary response to his touch, even when his fingers probed a tender spot close to her temple.

When she flinched he parted her hair and looked closely. 'The bruise is more dramatic than I expected—you must have hit yourself harder than you thought. But as you said yesterday it's still not much of a bump,' he said mockingly, releasing her and straightening as he stepped back. 'Is that what gave you the idea for this ludicrous charade, Aline?'

Fiercely resentful of his effortless domination, Aline stiffened her spine, refusing to let him see how terrified she was.

'It's certainly not enough of a bump to cause concussion,' he continued relentlessly. 'That leaves alcoholic amnesia—a blackout, in other words. You had one glass of champagne at the christening party.' Irony pulled his mouth straight. 'Yes, I was watching you. It's a habit I seem to have acquired lately. A single drink, followed by another two, drunk very slowly several hours later with food, wouldn't black out memory. It wouldn't even be enough to temporarily sap your will-power.'

Heat burned her skin again, but she kept her gaze fixed doggedly on him.

'Have you got a headache?'

She bit her lip. 'A slight one,' she admitted.

He went on in an insultingly reasonable tone, 'Probably not enough sleep.'

Cold with anguish, she said in a shaking voice, 'I don't remember how I got this bump. I am not trying to deceive you.' But inside she was crying, Am I that sort of person—lying, manipulative, cowardly? Surely not?

Pinning her down her with those cold predator's eyes, Jake went on judicially, 'Of course, intense emotional trauma is a possibility. You've been a devoted widow for almost three years—no lovers, not even a mild flirtation, so I'm told.' His eyelids drooped. 'What did I say? Ah, have there been lovers? Are you just very discreet, Aline?'

Even as she tried desperately to cling to it, the faint trace of a thought disappeared into the void from which it had come. Tears threatened to clog Aline's throat, but she squared her shoulders and chin against the crackle of danger in the air and said stubbornly, 'I can't remember.'

He paused, tigerish eyes glinting with some emotion she couldn't fathom. Harshly he said, 'Well, remember this. You agreed to come here, and last night you were the one who made the moves.' He nodded across the room to a chair. Startling against the cream upholstery, tossed by some casual hand, was a black bra, silkily transparent. On the floor lay another small pool of material and a pair of trousers.

'I didn't take the bra off,' Jake Howard said mockingly, and walked out of the room.

Aline sank back against the pillows, thinking sickly that she'd never wake up again without remembering this sordid humiliation.

Then she clamped her jaw tight and flung the bedclothes back, because memory was the one thing she didn't have.

The house had been built almost on the beach; to each side there were pohutukawa trees, their dark leaves lightened by bunches of silver buds. Which meant, Aline knew, that it would soon be summer, when New Zealand's most beautiful flowering tree burst into crimson and scarlet and burgundy tassels, so many that the huge trees shimmered with colour against the sea.

Swiftly she dragged her gaze from the view. Her eyes skidded over a breakfast setting in one of the windows, two finely woven cane chairs and a table—the chairs large enough to comfortably take Jake Howard's big, graceful body. His very size was intimidating, but the aura of power and forcefulness that clung to him truly worried her. He didn't look like a man it was wise to cross.

Had he planned to sit opposite her in that window and eat breakfast in some post-coital haze of satiation? Had she agreed?

And was he telling the truth when he said she'd 'made the moves'?

Cold with shame, Aline dragged the sheet from the bed and wound it around her body. Was that the sort of person she was? Provocative, forward, brassy? Nausea clutched her stomach.

No; he'd said she'd been a devoted widow. But her stiffness told her she'd been well and truly loved the previous night. And unless he'd kidnapped her, which didn't seem likely, she must have agreed to stay here with him.

Aline hurried across the room to the other door. It opened into a bathroom and a large, walk-in wardrobe. She peered into the wardrobe, sucking in her breath as she saw a casually chic weekend bag stacked against the wall, silent admission that she'd wanted this tryst as much as Jake had.

Slowly, gingerly, she stepped into the wardrobe. Hanging on the racks and stacked neatly on the shelves were clothes entirely suitable to a holiday at the beach—cotton shorts and wraps, T-shirts, a bathing suit in an intense turquoise blue and several sturdier garments in case the weather turned chilly.

Oh, yes, she'd definitely intended to stay here. Urgently she raced across and opened the bag, but it was empty of anything that hinted at her life.

Disappointment slammed into her. Sick with it, she found herself blinking back tears as she closed the case, clicked the catches together and set it against the wall, standing up to stare blankly around the room.

Only then did she notice that there were no men's clothes in the wardrobe.

So Jake had been telling the truth; he hadn't planned to share this bedroom.

Humiliation crawling unpleasantly through her, she walked into the bathroom. Her gaze flew to the mirror, her breath sighing out in intense relief when she recognised the face that stared back at her. Until then she hadn't realised how afraid she'd been that a stranger would stare at her from the mirror.

'Oh, thank God,' she muttered, checking out eyes the dense, vivid blue of turquoise, almond-shaped and widely set, transparent skin, black lashes and brows, and hair hanging in a sooty curtain halfway down her back.

Ignoring the frisson of apprehension down her spine, she unwound the sheet and surveyed her body gravely in the full-length mirror. It too held no surprises—she knew her white skin, the long, slender legs and arms, the small, neat breasts above a narrow waist and hips. No children, she decided, checking for stretch marks.

An upwelling sadness caught her totally by surprise. She almost surrendered to it, but only for a moment. Once more her chin came up, though she flushed at evidence of the night before—a slight reddening here and there of her translucent skin—and recalled the scratches on Jake's back.

If only she could remember!

'Trying to force it probably won't help,' she muttered, turning from the sight of those betraying marks to set the shower going.

But what if her memory never came back? What if she went through the rest of her life like this? Panic shook her; gripping the edge of the bench she bowed over it, shuddering like a tree in a cyclone.

Eventually she fought it back and straightened. She had to get away from Jake Howard and back to real life; the clues to her memory lay there, not in his luxurious house by the sea where she'd apparently enjoyed a night of decadence with him.

Walking into a strong, warm blast of water, she grabbed soap and facecloth and proceeded to scrub every bit of that night off her body.

When she emerged, pink all over, she towelled the water from her body with swift, ungentle hands. She didn't notice the handbag until she stooped to dry her feet. The same intense blue as her eyes, it lay open on its side behind the door.

Aline froze. 'Yes!' she whispered, because this would tell her so much.

With trembling hands she picked it up and shook out the contents.

Not much cash, although the wallet held a couple of gold credit cards and a chequebook. She stared at her signature, blinking away the easy tears when she didn't recognise it.

Her fingers went automatically to the pocket that held her driving licence; from it stared a solemn photograph in which she looked all of the twenty-eight years she apparently was. She'd been born on the sixteenth of November.

There wasn't much else—no old letters, nothing that gave her any handle on Aline Connor, not even a shopping list. Apparently she travelled light, and she was tidy. For the second time in a few minutes sick disappointment overwhelmed her with painful, almost physical ferocity.

'Stop this at once!' she told herself wearily. No doubt, in whatever home she inhabited, there was an everyday bag that held much more information than this one.

She stood with the bag clutched to her chest. 'Home,' she said aloud, tasting the word.

An overwhelming revulsion shocked her. Why? More quick, weak tears glimmered in her eyes; if only she had some slight inkling of her life, of the sort of person Aline Connor was. These sudden, baseless mood swings were probably entirely natural, given the situation, but they exhausted her and stopped her from thinking sensibly.

Setting the bag down on the marble bench, she wiped her eyes and snatched up the bath sheet, draping it around herself like a sarong before heading for the wardrobe.

She dumped the bag onto a shelf and began to dress, filled with determination. Today she'd leave this beach house, and the man who owned it, and go home to find herself again. At home there'd be letters she could read, and books and music and pictures she'd bought, invitations—all the paraphernalia necessary to jump-start her memory.

And what, a coldly logical part of her brain asked, if nothing helps?

The thought smashed the fragile veneer of her confidence. Swallowing to ease the dryness of panic in her mouth and throat, she closed her eyes, but immediately forced them open. If going home didn't do the trick, she'd try medicine, drugs, hypnosis—anything.

But for now she'd go out in full battle array.

Setting her mouth, she buttoned up a cream cotton shirt over her jeans, rolling up the sleeves to just below her elbows. Back in the bathroom she dried her hair and brushed it. The photograph on her driver's licence had shown it caught back behind her head, but that seemed too formal for the beach.

'Oh, no, it's not,' she muttered.

Fortunately some memory divorced from her brain and seated in habit told her hands how to do her hair, just as it guided her through the process of making up her face. Both, she discovered, were quite easy to accomplish if she stopped trying to remember how and just let her mind drift.

When she was ready she damped down the fear that lurked at the back of her mind and stared gravely at her reflection. Lips softly coloured, skin sheltering behind a faint translucent film of foundation, eyes tactfully enhanced, she looked good. Not sexy, no—that was the last thing she wanted! It put her at too much of a disadvantage when Jake Howard looked at her with those compelling, knowledgeable eyes.

Cool, controlled reserve—that was what she needed to hide her almost overpowering panic.

Knotting a cream and blue scarf around her throat, she walked into the bedroom and hauled the bedclothes back. When she straightened a glimmer of gold on the tiles over by the window table caught her eye. It was a thin gold chain, intricately woven like a silk rope, with a small diamond winking from the clasp.

'What on earth are you doing on the floor?' she said out loud.

Embarrassment cracked her composure. Perhaps she'd wrenched it off in her haste to get rid of her bra the night before. Tensely she scooped it up and dropped it over her head, smoothing it into place as she left the room.

Jake was coming along a wide glassed-in corridor that looked out over the beach. He stopped and watched her walk towards him, something in his glance making her skin prickle with apprehension.

But all he said was, 'I've made breakfast.'

Her stomach chose just that second to gurgle embarrassingly. His brows lifted in a taunting glance. 'Listen to your body,' he advised, his tone making the subtext clear; he wasn't referring just to food.

She was totally unprepared for the swift out-thrust of his hand towards her throat. Nevertheless, her reactions were fast—she'd almost jumped out of reach before his other hand closed around her shoulder.

'What do you think you're doing?' she gasped, held still in a merciless grip. She stared up into a face that shocked her—the predator with his prey fully in his sight, golden eyes darkening in barely suppressed rage.

Strong fingers caught the chain around her neck, flicking it over her head.

'Leave that alone!' she commanded fiercely, grabbing at the gold links.

He said between his teeth, 'What sort of person are you? While you're in my house, after a night in my bed, you will not wear the chain he gave you.' He dropped it on the floor with cruel dismissiveness. 'Not against the skin I've kissed, the breasts I've caressed and tasted, around the throat that called my name when you climaxed in my arms. Pack him away where he belongs, Aline, in the past.'

Something tightened inside her in response to the inherent sensuality of his words, a sensuality counteracted by the stark anger that sent a frisson of fear spiralling through her.

She had gone along with Jake's interpretation of this whole situation. But what if he'd kidnapped her? What if he'd drugged her and then packed her bag and brought her here, knowing that the drugs would leave her temporarily disoriented?

Even as she cringed at such feverish fantasies, she told herself that it wouldn't hurt to be careful.

Hot with angry fear, she stammered, 'I'm not... I didn't...'

'Of course you did,' he said coolly, releasing her with

a contemptuous abruptness. 'I want you, yes, but not as a substitute for a man you can't have because he's dead.'

She swallowed, her eyes held captive by the hard condemnation in his. Trying hard to make her voice steady, she said, 'Jake, I want to go home.'

The condemnation faded, replaced by what she sensed was unwilling sympathy. He touched her cheek and murmured in a low voice, 'Don't look so scared, darling heart.' His mouth twisted. 'Didn't last night show you that you have nothing to be afraid of? If it didn't, then I'll just have to prove it over and over until you're convinced.'

Astonished and appalled by her humiliating desire to be convinced, she hesitated.

Jake gave a slow smile. Perhaps there was a hint of calculation in it, but when she stared gravely at him it vanished. If it had ever been there. 'Come and have some breakfast.'

Her mind buzzing with indecision and apprehension, she nodded. 'All right,' she said meaninglessly, and went with him to the kitchen.

The house had been built with the short passage to her bedroom leading off a large living and dining-room. On the far side of the room another door hinted at other rooms. The stamp of the creative expert who'd furnished her bedroom was also evident here in the same sophisticated casualness and neutral shades of honey and sand and cream.

The soothing, homely bubble of coffee and the scent of toast indicated breakfast.

'How do you like your eggs?' Jake asked.

She hesitated, then said quietly, 'I don't know.'

Jake thought cynically that for a clever, disciplined woman, who'd fought her way to a position of considerable power, she was making a total hash of pretending to lose her memory. He wasn't a gambler, but he'd be prepared to bet a considerable amount of money that she'd been just about to tell him exactly how she liked her eggs when that cool, clear brain of hers had warned her it wouldn't look good.

Turning away, he cracked eggs into the pan and said aloud, 'Then I'll do them the same as mine—with the whites set.'

'Thank you,' she said in a muted voice.

When had she decided to wipe out the whole evening and return them both to square one?

Probably the instant she'd woken up and seen him in bed beside her. He had to admire her quick wits and her intelligence, even though he wanted to force her into accepting that last night had changed everything.

Frustration rode him; she'd been so bloody elusive, sliding with enigmatic grace past all his lures. He'd diluted his urgent male desire to hunt her down with every ounce of caution he possessed, and last night he'd thought he'd finally won his prize.

At the memory of her in his arms heat clamoured through him, storming the cold logic of his brain.

Yet last night had not been enough to get her out of his system; in spite of her wholesale surrender, he still wanted her with a primitive hunger that ate at his control and his strength. And although he wasn't going to let her get away with this charade, he'd better remember that she could be dangerous.

'Over there,' he said, nodding in its direction, 'is a toaster. Do you think you could put some bread in it?'

The soft glow of her skin suddenly faded into pallor. She was good; he had to admit it. Had she been acting last night? The thought knotted his gut and rasped in his voice. 'Give it up, Aline. Be honest—if you don't want an affair with me say so.'

'I don't want an affair with you,' she returned, almost stumbling over the words to add even more rapidly, 'I'm sorry if I—if I said that I would. I truly can't remember.'

Her white, brittle pride infuriated him so much that he

wanted to smash it into fragments. No other woman had ever been able to churn his emotions into custard. He gave a harsh laugh. 'Oh, forget it.'

Anger tightened inside him when he saw the relief she couldn't hide as she dropped bread into the toaster. What the hell was it about her that so unmanned him? She was beautiful, yes, with a disciplined, snow queen loveliness that had caught his eye the first time he'd seen her across a boardroom table.

But he'd made love to other beautiful women without this deep-seated hunger to possess and protect and cherish. And for every one he'd taken he'd rejected another politely. Jake had no illusions; he'd been born with a face that attracted women even before his bank balance had grown enough to cover any sort of physical or temperamental flaw. Women wanted security for all sorts of reasons rooted in humanity's past, and when they looked at him they saw a good provider.

But Aline Connor had made it obvious right from the start that she wanted neither him nor any security he could offer.

The coffee-maker bubbled in urgent signal. He picked it up and poured the steaming liquid into a couple of mugs. 'Sugar and milk?'

'I don't know how I have it.'

She said it defiantly, but he thought he detected a thread of fear in the words, and again felt that strange compulsion to protect her.

Something about this composed, elusive woman, still in thrall to her dead husband's memory, shattered his carefully crafted defences. Perhaps he'd grown arrogant because he'd never wanted a woman he couldn't have.

And perhaps, he thought with disciplined assurance as he poured milk into the cup, he was ignoring the one thing he had in his favour. In spite of her implacable resistance, she did want him. She might be the best actor in the world, but her body spoke a language he understood. From the moment they'd met she'd been acutely, anxiously aware of him, and last night she'd gone up in his arms like flames.

So she was regretting it now; well, he didn't have to make it easy for her to forget.

CHAPTER FIVE

PUSHING a mug across the counter, Jake said, 'Here, you look as though you could do with this.'

A confused torment of sensation exploded Aline's surface composure into shards. Assailed by an intense shaft of need, strong and uncontrollable, at the sight of him, she couldn't have spoken if her life had depended on it.

At least he now had clothes on!

Yet even without clothes he'd projected a formidable authority. A complex man; although he'd been scornful and contemptuous, sure her memory loss was some kind of sick ploy, he hadn't tried to pressure her. Picking up the mug, she gave him a quick glance from beneath her lashes. She couldn't imagine him trying to pressure anyone: he wouldn't need to. Bone-deep mastery of himself and any situation radiated from him.

'Most women seem to prefer toast or fruit for breakfast,' he remarked, 'but I know you like bacon and eggs.' He slid the eggs onto a dish, reached into the oven for another dish of bacon, and carried both through into the combined living and dining-room, a large open area with comfortable, casually elegant furniture.

Following him, coffee mug in hand, Aline asked warily, 'Have we eaten breakfast together before?'

'Not after a night of passion,' he said with a cool nonchalance that made her blink, walking through bifold doors that opened out onto a wide, wooden deck.

She persisted, 'Then when?'

Although he directed an impatient look at her, he answered briefly, 'Breakfast meetings, Aline.' And added mockingly, 'Before each round of negotiations.'

He had such a powerful impact on her it seemed impossible that those other meetings had been wiped from her mind overnight. She ignored the niggle of pain at her temple to ask, 'What sort of negotiations?'

'High finances,' he said in a level voice, more forbidding than if he'd shouted. 'Between us we negotiated a joint venture with a tribe from one of the Solomon Islands. We're setting up a plantation system on part of their land so they have a continued income. As well, we've agreed to help set up a small cosmetic oil industry. The bank you work for was retained by their government to do the negotiations.'

Following him along the deck, Aline opened her mouth to ask for more, met measuring tawny eyes, and thought better of it. Nothing he said had any personal implication for her, so any further information would be useless. But at least she now knew she worked for a bank.

The table, sheltered from the sun by a glossy-leaved vine, was set with linen and china in the same subtle, beachy colours as the furnishings. 'This is lovely. Very *House and Garden* chic,' she said, trying to sound normal and ordinary.

Jake set the dishes down and gave her a smile in which mockery and amusement were nicely blended. 'Said with the right patrician sneer. The decorator did a good job, although I'd prefer a little more warmth.'

Undercurrents in his tone, in his words—in the way his enigmatic, hooded eyes locked onto her mouth for a second before flicking up to capture her gaze—sent a swift quiver down her spine.

Feeling that she'd woken up in some alien dimension, where truth was turned on its head and threats lurked behind innocent words, Aline sat down in the chair he indicated. After a moment's indecision she lifted the mug of coffee and drank deeply; it took all of her self-control to stop her hands from shaking.

'Did I frighten you when I took the chain off?' Jake asked crisply, eyes narrowing as he looked at her.

'Yes, you scared me,' she said. Her throat where the chain had rested felt bereft, as empty as her mind. 'You meant to.'

He lowered himself into the chair opposite her before saying, 'I'm sorry—my reaction was over the top. Put it down to a certain male arrogance.'

'I already had,' she returned crisply. Startled and suspicious of his low laughter, she looked up into eyes that blazed like crystals. 'What's so funny about that?'

'I like the way you give no quarter,' he said lazily, adding with the unexpectedness of a striking snake, 'Drop the amnesia bit, Aline, it's not worthy of you. We can work things out without that.'

Suddenly furious, she flared, 'I am *not* making it up.'

He gave a lazy, insolent smile. 'Coward.' When she didn't answer he drawled, 'Don't you want any breakfast?'

What small appetite she'd had was gone, but she'd be stupid not to eat something. 'Of course I do. This looks wonderful,' she said automatically and insincerely, sounding, she realised too late, like a child reminded of its manners.

Jake said on a hard, sardonic note, 'I haven't poisoned it. Serve yourself, sprinkle with pepper and salt, pick up your knife and fork, cut up the eggs and bacon, chew them and swallow.'

She threw him a fiery glance, hoping he couldn't see the panicky desolation behind it. 'I know how to eat.'

Once more that low laughter took her completely by surprise. 'You've got a nice line in female arrogance,' he said smoothly. 'We're a lot alike, you and I.'

Suppressing a wild response to the taunting invitation of his smile, Aline began to eat with studious concentration.

It should have been pleasant to sit at the sunny table

and listen to the call of seabirds and the soothing murmur of the wavelets on the beach. Eating was such everyday, humdrum behaviour; especially breakfast. Its very ordinariness should have calmed her.

Instead, her nerves were fraying, her body was betraying her with acute awareness, and the silence had somehow assumed a huge significance. Sex, she decided bitterly, had a lot to answer for—it had forged an intense physical intimacy that still held in spite of her locked mind.

Uneasily she wondered if she really did want to remember what had happened the previous night. Had he been tender or wildly exciting? A contraction in the pit of her stomach warned her that she'd better get off this subject and fast, leaving any forgotten sins safely hidden in the darkness of her mind.

Tender or not, making love to Jake would have been— overwhelming, like being claimed by a storm.

Aline chewed stubbornly on. The bacon was crisp, the eggs delicious, yet she had to force them down.

Jake had gathered half a dozen scarlet flowers from the large bush just outside on the terrace and dropped them carelessly onto the table. They lay like silk ornaments on the cloth, gold-tipped, flagrantly beautiful.

Suddenly eager to break the taut silence, she reached over and touched one, her fingers lingering against a petal. 'These are so pretty,' she said.

'That's interesting.'

She jerked back her hand as though stung by a lurking bee. 'Why?'

'Hibiscuses are flamboyant and theatrical, real no-holds-barred flowers. Very much at odds with that very composed face you present to the world.' His voice was neutral, but she looked up into uncomfortably penetrating eyes.

Gritting her teeth, she gave him a polite, dismissive smile. 'But beautiful. No one could dislike them.'

'What are your favourite flowers?'

'I don't know,' she said briefly. Frowning, she picked up a bloom, holding it in the palm of her hand and keeping her gaze fixed on the elaborate silken ruffles. She couldn't remember liking flowers; she couldn't remember anything, she thought with a flash of near-hysterical terror that warned her to think of something else.

'What are your favourites?' she asked.

He paused before saying dryly, 'I like gardenias. I enjoy the contrast between the demure colour and the heavy, almost cloying perfume and the incredible texture of the petals, like the finest velvet. They're very sensuous flowers.'

Something in his voice set off warning bells. 'They sound it,' she said unevenly. His words brought no pictures to her mind, but she'd remember that he loved gardenias. And she would also remember that these were hibiscuses. Waking up with an empty brain didn't mean it had to stay that way.

A black eyebrow climbing, he surveyed her face with leisurely, intimidating thoroughness. 'Eat up. You don't look as though you've had a decent meal for a while.'

Aline looked down at her arms, infuriatingly familiar. From some unknown place inside her came an imprudent response. 'Am I too thin?'

His gaze roamed her with slow thoroughness, setting off tiny explosions of sensation throughout her body. 'No.' His voice didn't change but she responded with involuntary excitement to the pulse of sexuality beneath the word. 'I was referring to a certain air of fragility that's so much a part of you everyone seems to ignore it.'

Who was *everyone?* Once again, panic stirred, threatening to drag her down into its murky, unreasoning depths. Sickly, she realised that in all the world Jake Howard was the only person she knew.

She thrust the thought to the back of her mind. Later

she'd deal with it; for now she had to continue this duelling dance of advance and retreat.

'I feel as strong as a horse,' she said crisply, picking up the knife and fork again. If he said anything more about her fragility with that disturbing, equivocal note in his voice her throat would close up entirely.

Jake's perceptive, burnished eyes must have noted her withdrawal because for the rest of the meal he contented himself with casual, almost detached conversation. Gratefully, Aline followed suit, startled to find herself fighting a sense of rightness, of companionability, almost more difficult to bear than her outrageous physical reaction to him.

It had to be because she'd eaten breakfast like this with her husband—the husband she couldn't remember.

The toast, delicately brown and crunchy, spread with marmalade that clamped onto her tastebuds with satisfying impact, turned to cardboard in her mouth. Ignoring a glass of freshly squeezed orange juice, she drank the rest of her coffee.

When they'd finished the meal and cleared the table he eyed her with a frown. 'You're still a bit pale. Come for a walk.' At her momentary hesitation he gave a hard smile. 'I won't touch you.'

And because she wanted to get out of the house and away from the spurious intimacy of that tumbled bed, she said, 'A walk sounds an excellent idea.'

With a bite in his voice, he said, 'Have you decided I'm trustworthy, Aline?'

Had she? She didn't know enough about him to trust him—but a purely female instinct accepted that he wouldn't hurt her. 'So far,' she returned uncertainly.

He gave her a mocking glance. 'I'm relieved.'

Together they walked across the springy grass of the lawn and down a couple of steps onto the beach. The sun beat down, teasing them with its promise of summer's generosity. Determined to keep her eyes away from the man who strode lithely beside her, Aline stared out across the dancing, glinting waters of the little bay as she set off over the thick, soft sand.

Something hard beneath the clinging surface caught one foot. With a startled yelp, she flung her hands out to break her landing, but before she hit the sand Jake caught her in a grip of iron, jerking her away from the spiky log her incautious kick had found.

'I'm all right,' she said raggedly, senses humming at his closeness, the strength of his hands around her waist, the quick lift of his chest.

'Sure?' He looked down into her face, his own absorbed and intent.

'Yes,' she said breathlessly. 'It didn't hurt—I slipped off it. I'll take my shoes off—I like walking barefoot on the beach.'

'I'll do it.' Before she could protest, he let her go and crouched to untie the laces on her shoes.

Aline looked down at his bent black head, shimmering with tawny fire, and something moved in the pit of her stomach, something both erotic and emotion-laden. Shocked, she glanced away, and for a dazed moment the sun danced in the glowing sky while her strength seeped through the soles of her feet.

Instinctively she supported herself by clutching one broad shoulder. Her fingers curled and she thought that she could feel Jake's life force beating up into them, dynamic, aggressive, irresistible.

He looked up at her, narrowed golden eyes blazing. For a long tense moment their glances locked until in one powerful movement he stood up. 'Step out,' he ordered, a raw note underlining the words.

A single pace freed one foot; she took another and was at last far enough away from him to breathe properly. After clearing her throat she said stupidly, 'Thank you.'

'My pleasure.' He bent to slide off his own shoes.

That elusive feeling of rightness startled her again. To banish it she blurted the first thing that came to her head. 'Who did you get those astonishing eyes from?'

His brows lifted; shying his shoes onto the bank, he said, 'My mother.'

The shoes landed exactly where he'd aimed them. Well, naturally—not for nothing did he have that air of super-competence. Aline cleared her throat and said, 'I don't think I've ever met anyone with eyes that colour before.'

'Cats' eyes,' he said laconically, holding out his hand for her shoes.

She knew what cats were. Nodding, she took care to hand him the shoes without touching him

Her shoes followed his, landing beside them. Dusting the sand from his fingers, he turned to look at her. Although the sun shone full in his face, she couldn't read his expression when he said dryly, 'Where did you get yours from?'

'My father,' she said automatically, then stopped, her heart jumping. How did she know that? It had come from nowhere, that single fact. Confused, she set off along the beach, ignoring the bite of the hot sand on her tender soles.

No wonder Jake thought she was playing games with him!

'Your father?' he said neutrally from beside her. 'At first I thought you wore contact lenses to intensify their colour.'

'Why would I do that?'

He gave her a considering, sideways glance. 'To impress. It didn't take me long to realise that you don't care what effect you have on men. Your natural sense of style means that you always dress elegantly, but everything about your attitude proclaims that you aren't trying to attract.'

Aline stiffened, sensing condemnation beneath his detached tone. 'I wear make-up,' she retorted, striving not to sound defensive.

'With subtlety and restraint, carefully chosen—like your tasteful clothes—to play down your sexuality,' he returned with caustic, uncompromising detachment. 'You walk into every room, every situation, every social occasion, carrying a keep-off sign.'

That stung, as he'd meant it to. 'Is that why you want me?' she demanded angrily. 'Because I'm not easy?'

The pause that followed her injudicious question lifted the hair on the back of her neck. Apparently she'd been pathetically easy.

Finally he drawled, 'Most boys grow out of that sort of mindless point-scoring by the time they leave high school. I certainly did. And the keep-off sign meant nothing—I rarely take people at their own valuation. You revealed yourself as a closet sensualist time and time again.'

'How?' She should be wary—she *was* wary!—yet she was also intensely stimulated by the conversation. By everything, she amended hastily. Surely some of this blazing anticipation was due to the glorious day, the scent of the sea, the way the birds swooped and dived and called overhead...

Don't lie, she told herself ruthlessly. You don't care about the birds or the sea—you're entirely focused on Jake Howard, who is a stranger, even if he has been kind as well as forbidding.

Even if you did spend last night in bed with him...

'How did you give yourself away? You eat with enjoyment,' he said, watching her with clinical objectiveness. 'You respond openly and ardently to beauty. I've seen you sit at a concert with tears in your eyes. And you like children. Yesterday at Emma's christening you cuddled her for half an hour. She obviously knows you well and likes you very much. You're a very sensuous woman, Aline. I was already convinced of that before last night.'

Colour drummed up through her skin. 'How gratifying to be right.'

It gave her angry enjoyment to see his cheekbones darken. However, his eyes gleamed and his beautiful mouth curved in a sudden, sexy smile that sent shivers of excitement across her skin.

'You enjoyed making love last night,' he said, his voice low and lazy and caressing. 'Almost as much as I did.'

Without looking at him she swallowed, and forced a brisk practicality into her voice. It didn't work; to her horror the words emerged in husky hesitancy. 'How long have we known each other?'

After a deliberate moment he said, 'You know it's been a couple of months.'

For some reason she asked, 'Do I know your mother?'

'No,' he said briefly. 'She died when I was eight.'

'I'm so sorry,' Aline said, thinking how inadequate such a trite phrase was. She ached to think of an eight-year-old boy weeping for his mother.

'It was twenty-seven years ago.'

'Eight is so young,' she said quietly. 'It must have left a huge hole in your life.'

'Yes.' He walked down to the water, picked up a small round stone and shied it, watching it skip several times before sinking.

'Well done,' Aline congratulated solemnly.

He began walking again. 'My father taught me how to do that. A couple of years after my mother died he married again, and although his new wife was charming and affectionate she wasn't very old. She wanted to play rather than be responsible for a ten-year-old boy, so I was sent to boarding school.'

'That was cruel,' Aline said fiercely.

He turned his head, topaz eyes enigmatic. 'I enjoyed it. Don't pity me, Aline—that's not what I want from you. I knew my father loved me, and my stepmother did her best. We're good friends still.'

'No child should be sent off like an unwanted parcel.' Something clamped her heart at the idea of a schoolboy with his mother's eyes torn away from all he knew, all he held dear.

Startled by her reaction, she pointed at the elegant shape of a three-masted yacht slipping by at some distance. 'That's so beautiful! I wonder what it is.'

'It looks like one of the *Spirits*—the youth training ships. *Spirit of New Zealand,* I'd say. She's beating up the channel between us and the mainland; when she reaches that point there she'll go about and head into Auckland.'

'Between us and the mainland?' she echoed numbly, and stopped to stare about her. 'Is this an island?'

Frowning, he said grimly, 'You know it's an island.'

Something stirred behind that curtain across her brain. Racked by a violent hope, she tried to force it out of the mists, but as she groped it faded into darkness. She said despairingly, 'I don't remember anything about an island.'

He surveyed her with eyes as unreadable as polished gilt. 'I thought you didn't remember anything,' he said cruelly.

Frustration and fear thinned her voice. 'Just a snatch— a floating fragment—now and then. And then it goes.' Even to her own ears it sounded lame. Swallowing hard, she asked, 'How long did we plan to stay here?'

In an even voice that came close to being bored, he told her, 'A week.'

Aline shook her head. 'I've changed my mind. I want to go home.'

'We have no way of getting off the island.'

'What? You must have a boat—'

'Stop it, Aline,' he said harshly. 'You know damned well we came by helicopter. I don't have a boat here, not even a dinghy.'

'Then I'll swim,' she cried, desperation driving her to rashness as she swirled around and took a couple of steps towards the sea.

He brought her up short with an ungentle hand around her wrist. 'How do you know you can swim?' he asked, not trying to hide the taunting disbelief in his voice.

She returned angrily, 'I—don't, but I can find out. Let me go, damn you!' She gave her wrist a jerk, but his fingers tightened, holding her firm.

'It's five miles to the mainland. However good a swimmer you are—' his eyes assessed her shoulders and upper arms, dismissing her chances of being any sort of swimmer '—the currents in the gulf are dangerous.' When she stared mutinously at him he stated, 'Don't try it, Aline.'

'I'm not—'

'If you want to die,' he said brutally, turning her to face him, lean fingers enclosing her wrist in a grip that hinted of steel, 'you can do it when I'm not around.'

'I don't want to die!'

'If you even look like doing something so criminally stupid,' he said with icy determination, 'I'll keep you safe if I have to shackle you to me.'

His fingers tightened a second. Unremembered fire surged high, needles of flame lancing through her, lighting an inferno inside. Aline lost herself in his half-closed gleaming eyes, and, in spite of the tension and her fear, excitement rose in a slow, merciless tide. Senses sharpening, she heard the increasing drumming of her heartbeat, saw the swift throb of the pulse at the base of his tanned throat, felt his strength and dynamic power beating against her.

He knows, she thought, trying to extinguish her chaotic responses. He knows I feel like this...

'Tell me you won't try to swim off the island,' he commanded, his lips barely moving.

Unable to tear her gaze away from his, she hesitated, but eventually muttered, 'Of course I won't risk my life.'

In a voice turned to iron by concentrated will-power, he said, 'I need that promise, Aline.'

'All right,' she agreed furiously, 'you have it. I won't try to swim to the mainland. Satisfied?'

'It will do to go on with,' he said without emotion, dropping her wrist as though her skin burned.

Aline began to pace back towards the house, her feet sinking into the dry sand. 'What on earth are we going to do for a week?' she demanded jerkily.

'You need a holiday—you've been working like a maniac.' His mouth hardened. 'And don't glower at me like that. I'm not interested in an unwilling woman.'

His words reminded her of the suspicion that had sneaked across her brain and been hastily banished because she couldn't bear to think of it. Cowardice, she realised now.

'So you say, but why should I believe you?' she asked, facing the ugly supposition head-on. 'For all I know, yesterday you might have slipped a drug in that glass of champagne I drank and brought me here against my will. Date rape happens.'

He didn't move. The sunlight that warmed them both suddenly darkened and vanished as a cloud slid across the sky. Aline hid a shiver; holding her head high, she searched his handsome, uncommunicative face.

'Anything's possible,' he said in a tone that lifted every tiny hair across her skin. Taking her by surprise with a sudden movement, he stripped his shirt over his head and swung around to expose the welts across his back, red and angry against his tanned skin. 'But the marks you put on me,' he said dangerously, 'are on my back, not on my face and chest where they'd be if I'd raped you. And I don't know of any drug that is both an aphrodisiac and a memory-killer.' He pulled the shirt on again and turned to face her. 'Do you?'

Scarlet-faced, she held his gaze. Too much spoke in his favour—the suitcase packed with enough clothes to last a week was enough on its own—but she believed him because of an intangible trust that had nothing to do with facts. 'No,' she said curtly. 'Do you believe that I've lost my memory?'

After a crackling pause, he said, 'The jury's still out on that.'

'Why would I pretend such a stupid thing?' she cried desperately.

Black, thick lashes screened his eyes. 'I can think of several reasons. One being that you got cold feet at the idea of an affair with me.'

'If I changed my mind I'd just tell you,' she said desperately, 'not hide behind a stupid lie.'

He lifted his brows.

Struggling for composure, Aline looked behind him to the mainland, distant, unreachable. The compulsion to go back home, to find herself there, burned inside her. She said in a flat, unemphatic voice, 'You must be able to get off this place.'

'No,' Jake said brusquely.

'But you must have a way of contacting other people.'

'Why?'

'In case you need them—if you hurt yourself. A mobile phone…' Her voice trailed away as he reached out and traced along her cheekbone.

Astonished, she realised that she was weakening, her mastery of her will giving way before an unsubtle sexual chemistry. Their coupling the previous night, forgotten and bitterly regretted, had forged a physical connection between them that wouldn't be ignored.

But it could be leashed and controlled, she thought stoutly, refusing to flinch or pull away, wide eyes defiant as she met his half-closed ones. In a voice that cracked, she repeated, 'Surely you have a mobile telephone?'

'Bad reception makes it almost impossible to use one. I've already tried this morning.'

The sun returned, dappling the huge, sweeping branches of the trees behind the beach. 'What about a computer—e-mail?' she asked quickly.

'Nothing,' Jake said brusquely. 'You wanted to be out of touch.' Something altered in his tone. In a swift movement he wrapped a hand around the back of her neck.

He didn't use his great strength to pull her any closer, but if he decided to she'd have no chance of fighting him off.

'You're marooned here with me, Aline.' His voice dropped. 'So what are you going to do about it, darling heart?'

'Don't call me that,' she snarled, refusing to acknowledge the rapid pumping of her heart and the way her nostrils flared delicately at the faint scent of aroused male.

'Why not? You didn't mind last night,' he taunted.

She lost her temper, shouting, 'I don't *remember* last night, damn you!'

'Remember it or not, it happened,' he said insolently. 'You made love as though you'd been starved for years, all your life, like a wildcat, calling my name as you writhed in my arms. If it meant nothing, why deny yourself?'

'Because you're a stranger to me! I'm not going to sleep with a man I don't know,' she hissed, reining in her temper with an effort that glittered in her eyes. 'And perhaps it was an aberration, something I regret and am ashamed of. Perhaps that's why I woke up this morning unable to remember it! Whatever, I'm not going to—to repeat it.'

Although his expression didn't alter, she sensed a concealed threat. Before she had time to do more than draw her breath he let her go, wiping his hands as though touching her had left them covered in slime.

He said indifferently, his tone hard and contemptuous, 'In that case, as neither of us can get off the island, I suggest you put aside your chagrin at behaving for once like an ordinary human being with ordinary human needs and desires, and settle down to enjoy a holiday away from telephones and computers and journalists.'

Something nagged at her, something she couldn't put a finger on. 'It looks as though I'll have to,' she said sullenly.

'Don't sulk,' he said without trying to moderate the sarcasm in his tone. 'Think of it as a rest.'

'Doing what?' she demanded, frustration and anger riding her. 'Quarrelling?'

His burnished gaze mocked her. 'There are plenty of books to read. You can swim if I'm around. I'll even teach you to cook if you want to. But, judging by those shadows under your eyes, you need sleep most. Why don't you have a swim now and then try for a nap? Breakfast was late—we can eat lunch when you wake.'

At least that gave some structure to the day—and would keep her out of his way! And the water, still cool so early in the season, might help jog her brain into action. 'Yes,' she said crisply, setting out for the bach, 'a swim sounds like a good idea.'

Back at the house, she escaped into the bedroom and got into her bathing suit, a sleek one-piece. On, it looked far too brief, and gave undue prominence to her breasts and legs, but she found a wrap in the same material; after winding it around her hips and draping a towel across one shoulder in what she hoped was an insouciant fashion, she left the bedroom.

The house rang with a silence that told her Jake wasn't inside. Her eyes caught by movement in the bay, she stopped on the edge of the deck. Unwillingly she watched, admiring his long arms cutting smoothly through the water.

He was a very physical man, his body impressive in its promise of power and energy. Unfortunately, his face revealed intelligence and determination and a bone-deep discipline that probably came from his early years. And with it all he was utterly disturbing and compelling, she thought, fire flickering through her again.

A flash of white caught her attention; a yacht sailed around the point, its sails dipping as the wind caught it. If only she could signal to it...

Without thinking, she dragged the wrap free of her hips and raced out onto the crisp grass, frantically waving the blue material in great sweeps from side to side.

CHAPTER SIX

THE sailors waved back cheerfully before the yacht went about and veered towards the distant mainland.

Sick with disappointment, Aline stood with the cloth clutched in her hands, watching the sails disappear behind the next headland while Jake swam ashore and walked out of the sea, big body shimmering golden, a potent mixture of sunlight and water gilding and highlighting every coil and flexion of muscle as he walked through the soft sand.

Aline's disappointment vanished as adrenalin and a pang of exquisite, forbidden hunger sizzled through her.

Why deny yourself? His taunting words echoed in her ears. He bent to grab a towel from the sand, slinging it over his shoulder in one smooth movement as he came purposefully towards her. Lifting her chin, she met the tawny irony in his gaze.

He'd seen her as soon as she emerged from the house, every curve of her graceful body outlined by the sarong. And swimming as fast and as far as he could hadn't eased the slashing gripe of need a bit.

A purely territorial impulse, aggressive and unvarnished, had brought him back to land. His body tightened in a prowling, primal hunger.

She looked as she always looked—bandbox-fresh, cool, totally in control. From the first moment he'd seen her he'd wanted to ruffle that exclusive, prim neatness, discover for himself if the breasts that pushed so pertly against her silk shirts were as responsive as her lush mouth promised.

Well, last night he'd found out; to his incredulous pleasure she'd been ferociously female, wilder and more demanding than he'd ever hoped for.

And where had it got him?

'Right back to square one,' he said satirically, coming to a stop.

Her arched brows rose. 'Who is?'

Ruthlessly he squelched images from the previous night when her voice had been husky with passion, when it had trembled as she'd touched him with eager astonishment...

'Both of us.' He tossed the towel onto the grass and smiled at her, saw her eyes widen, the muscles tighten in her throat. 'You're so scared you're hiding behind a fake loss of memory, and I'm so hard I'm not decent.' With savage satisfaction he watched colour flood her translucent skin. 'We're right back to where we were months ago when I saw you across a boardroom table and wanted you.'

Although she managed to keep her eyes steadily on his, he knew the effort it took. Silently she turned and walked away from him, dropping her towel and the wrap onto the sand.

Jake cursed quietly and without satisfaction as she waded into the water and dived. Frowning, he waited until her black head broke the surface, relaxing subtly when he saw that she swam strongly with the inherent grace particularly hers, her expensive suit hiding nothing of the sleek body it made a pretence at covering.

She was running scared, retreating from him as fast as she could.

He wasn't going to let her get away with it.

Aline swam until heavy limbs drove her ashore. Although Jake, lounging in one of the oversize steamer chairs on the wide terrace, appeared to be concentrating on a book, she didn't make the mistake of thinking he wasn't keeping a close watch on her.

On the beach again, she turned her back to the house and submitted gratefully to the sun's ministrations, almost purring as warmth soaked into her. The wash of water past her skin had heightened her senses, transforming her body into something painfully taut and eager and consumed by a dangerous anticipation.

'You'll burn,' Jake said from behind her.

She swivelled, to see him standing a few feet away. His glance swept her pale shoulders before lifting to her mouth, resting there for a significant moment.

Staking a claim, she thought confusedly. He was crowding her, reminding her that they'd made love the previous night. 'I'll go inside and change shortly.'

'Now,' he said pleasantly.

Fuming, Aline straightened up, pushing wet hair back from her face. Holding his eyes with her own, she said just as pleasantly, 'Go to hell,' and walked past him, spine stiff, shoulders held so rigid that every muscle protested.

His low laughter behind her set fire to her temper. Her long stride faltered but a fierce pride drove her on.

After she'd showered and dressed she stripped the bed with angry speed, bundling the sheets and pillowslips into a pile with the clothes she'd discarded the previous night.

The house was still quiet when she emerged, but she sensed Jake's presence, a dangerous energy in the air.

Common courtesy dictated that instead of searching for the laundry and the linen cupboard she ask where they were. Setting her jaw, she went out onto the terrace.

A book face-down on his lean stomach, he was lying back in the lounger apparently gazing out to sea. Or sleeping.

The sight of him sprawled in the shade couldn't affect her emotionally because she didn't know him. No, the sudden quickening of her breath had to be a meaningless female acknowledgment of his strong sexual charisma, a hint from her body that although she didn't recall their lovemaking, it was imprinted in her cells.

What else didn't she recall? Humiliating panic almost broke through her fragile composure. She hated feeling

GET FREE BOOKS and a FREE GIFT WHEN YOU PLAY THE...

Just scratch off the silver box with a coin. Then check below to see the gifts you get!

SLOT MACHINE GAME!

YES! I have scratched off the silver box. Please send me the 2 free Harlequin Presents® books and gift for which I qualify. I understand I am under no obligation to purchase any books, as explained on the back of this card.

306 HDL DRRK

106 HDL DRRZ
(H-P-01/03)

FIRST NAME   LAST NAME

ADDRESS

APT.#   CITY

STATE/PROV.   ZIP/POSTAL CODE

7	7	7	**Worth TWO FREE BOOKS plus a BONUS Mystery Gift!**
🍒	🍒	🍒	**Worth TWO FREE BOOKS!**
♣	♣	♣	**Worth ONE FREE BOOK!**
🔔	🔔	🔔	**TRY AGAIN!**

Visit us online at www.eHarlequin.com

DETACH AND MAIL CARD TODAY!

The Harlequin Reader Service® — Here's how it works:

Accepting your 2 free books and gift places you under no obligation to buy anything. You may keep the books and gift and return the shipping statement marked "cancel." If you do not cancel, about a month later we'll send you 6 additional books and bill you just $3.57 each in the U.S., or $4.24 each in Canada, plus 25¢ shipping & handling per book and applicable taxes if any.* That's the complete price and — compared to cover prices of $4.25 each in the U.S. and $4.99 each in Canada — it's quite a bargain! You may cancel at any time, but if you choose to continue, every month we'll send you 6 more books, which you may either purchase at the discount price or return to us and cancel your subscription.

*Terms and prices subject to change without notice. Sales tax applicable in N.Y. Canadian residents will be charged applicable provincial taxes and GST.

If offer card is missing write to: Harlequin Reader Service, 3010 Walden Ave., P.O. Box 1867, Buffalo NY 14240-1867

BUSINESS REPLY MAIL
FIRST-CLASS MAIL   PERMIT NO. 717-003   BUFFALO, NY

POSTAGE WILL BE PAID BY ADDRESSEE

HARLEQUIN READER SERVICE
3010 WALDEN AVE
PO BOX 1867
BUFFALO NY 14240-9952

NO POSTAGE
NECESSARY
IF MAILED
IN THE
UNITED STATES

vulnerable—it terrified and antagonised her. Coolly, baldly, she said his name.

His black head turned; lazy, half-hidden eyes scanned her with something very close to insolence. 'Yes?' he said indolently.

She needed every advantage she could gain to deal with this man. Briefly she fought a wild desire to challenge his unfaltering self-assurance.

'Where's the laundry?' she asked, forcing the words into a calmly conversational mould. 'And where can I find some bed linen?'

His lashes drooped. 'The laundry's beyond the kitchen, and the linen cupboard's in the corridor outside the bedroom.' He paused before drawling, 'Need help to make the bed?'

Tension sparked across her nerve-ends. Oh, he knew how to get to her! 'No, thank you,' she said in a tone too clipped to be safe or wise, and marched back into the house.

It helped slightly to fling the clothes and linen into the large washing machine, set the controls with short, vicious jabs and, when it whooshed into life, stride back through the house and yank open the door of the linen cupboard. Shelves of sheets in sun-kissed shades of sand and straw and driftwood met her infuriated eyes.

Clearly Jake's decorator had overlooked no touch that would emphasise the beach ambience.

With grim determination Aline chose linen and carried it into her room where she set about remaking the bed. The fresh sheets eased the frightening tension that seethed beneath her surface, and if that was illogical—well, a woman who had lost her memory was practically *obliged* to be illogical.

'There,' she said defiantly when it was done, smoothing the coverlet. Beneath her breath she muttered, 'That's exorcised you, Jake Howard.'

And knew she lied. Whenever she slept in this bed he'd be there with her.

A knock on the door jerked her upright. Mouth tightening into a straight line, she stared across the room, then walked over and pulled the door open. Jake stood in the hallway, broad of shoulder, narrow of hip, long-legged and dominant, his slow smile not softening his face.

In spite of his perfect bone-structure, nobody would ever have accused him of being magazine-model handsome. One glance at him proclaimed mental and emotional toughness backed by a steely intelligence that was a threat in itself.

And that disconcerting tinge of fire in the black hair suggested a temper behind his implacable self-possession. Even the way he moved—with the aggressive grace of a hunter, silently, every muscle coiled and alert—stated that this was a man to be wary of.

Infuriatingly, Aline had to swallow before she could say, 'Yes?'

'I thought you might like something to drink.'

She showed her teeth in a smile that wasn't conciliatory. 'I thought a nap was next on the programme.' And could have bitten out her tongue the moment the words left it.

Of all the idiotic things to say!

Unkind amusement glittered in the golden depths of his eyes and his mouth quirked, but he said evenly, 'I'm making myself a cup of coffee.'

Common sense nagged that they had seven days to get through; the time would go faster and more pleasantly if she was polite. Was she always so—so edgy and antagonistic? It was stupid to search his every word for ulterior motives—and the offer of a drink could hardly be more harmless.

Aline glanced at her watch and made up her mind. 'Tea would be lovely, thank you. Then I thought I'd go for a walk.'

The amusement deepened in his eyes, but he said blandly, 'Why not?'

After he'd switched on the kettle he showed her the book-lined hallway that led to the other bedrooms, saying, 'Borrow anything you like.'

Her gaze skimmed the shelves. 'A very eclectic collection,' she murmured, pulling out an impressive tome on the relationship between science and religion.

'I have wide interests,' he said, dead-pan. 'So do you.'

Hot-eyed, she stared at him.

Aline thrust the book back onto the shelf. 'I'll hang out the clothes.'

'Where had you planned to walk? If it's to the other side of the island it will take at least half an hour, and unless you don't mind retracing your footsteps over the hill we'll have to leave within twenty minutes to catch the tide right.'

Dismayed, she exclaimed, 'You don't need to come!'

'You'll want a guide,' he told her easily, lion-coloured eyes as enigmatic as his smile.

Aline clamped her lips shut, holding back the tumbling words while Jake surveyed her with more amusement. After a sizzling few seconds she said stiffly, 'Thank you.'

'My pleasure.' His arrogant face was as unreadable as his voice, but the words were laced with enough mockery to set her teeth well and truly on edge.

As she pegged the sheets onto the line outside the back door she decided angrily that he was working to some hidden agenda. It might only be to persuade her back into his bed, but she sensed uncompromising determination behind his cool self-assurance.

The week stretched in front of her like seven years.

They drank the tea out on the deck. Aline tried very hard to enjoy the silence and the warmth, the glitter of the ocean and the fresh, mingled scents of plants and salt. From somewhere close by some insect strummed its tiny zither, an oddly croaky noise that nevertheless soothed her jumpy nerves.

'Have you got a hat?' Jake asked lazily from the steamer chair. When she nodded, he went on, 'Sunscreen?'

'Yes, thank you.'

'Have you put it on?'

She got to her feet. 'I'll do it now,' she said, trying to sound reasonable, cheerful, composed, as though she was a normal woman and this a normal occasion.

As though she could remember who she was and how she'd got to be there; as though she hadn't made love with the man who watched her with such steady, ruthless patience.

When she came back she noticed the swift glance with which he checked her hat and the fact that she'd anointed herself with protection from New Zealand's notorious sun.

'Do you want to go along the coast first or over the hill?' he asked.

'Over the hill,' she said without thinking.

His mouth curled. 'Checking to make sure this is really an island?'

She flashed him a glittering smile. 'Of course.'

'Sensible woman,' he said lazily. 'One of the things I like about you is that you have a mind like a steel trap.'

A steel trap that was firmly closed against her, she thought, rattled by a gust of futile anger. 'For a moment I wondered if you were going to say I had a mind like a man,' she returned sweetly.

'Heard that before, have you?' He turned and walked through the glass door onto the deck.

Confused, she hesitated before following her gut instinct. 'Yes, I think I have.'

He glanced back, brilliant eyes gleaming. 'And you didn't like it?'

'It's not a compliment for any woman to be told she thinks like a man,' she said coolly. Thick grass clutched

her feet; walking across the lawn was like wading through
ankle-deep carpet until they reached the trees at the bottom
of the hill. 'It implies that women can't think "properly".'
She invested the last word with trenchant scorn.

'Women tend to think differently.'

'Why should that be considered inferior?'

'Because until very recently men made the rules,' he
said, and laughed at her snort. 'It's no use trying to pick
a fight with me, Aline. I agree that it's no compliment,
and the women in my organisation are valued for the same
things I value in the men—their ability to get results.
Watch your step here. The path tends to get overgrown
during the winter.'

Behind the house the low hill climbed steeply beneath
its cloak of native trees, a small remnant of the forest that
had clothed New Zealand before man came.

'You call this a path?' Aline asked dryly, hauling herself
up the first abrupt bank with the aid of a sturdy vine that
looped down from the heights. 'It looks like a creek bed.'

'In winter it is. Just be thankful it hasn't rained for a
couple of days,' Jake said, stepping aside so that she could
go ahead. 'Go on,' he said, when she stopped and stared
up at him. 'If you slip I'll catch you.'

'I won't slip.' She brushed past him.

As she climbed Jake watched the material of her trousers
stretch across a heart-shaped, very sexy backside.
Elemental instincts burned into an aching, desperate hunger; he had to stop his hands from reaching for her, his
mouth from claiming her, his body from stamping her as
his over and over again until she gave up this charade and
accepted what had happened between them.

He'd always known that in him the hunter was barely
hidden beneath a civilised veneer, but until he'd met Aline
Connor he'd found it relatively easy to curb his appetites.

Last night had blown that control to bits. Now whenever

he looked at her he felt like a sixteen-year-old again, barely able to leash his new-found lust.

Although he'd always liked restrained, intelligent women, what had first fired his alert interest in a beautiful woman into outright desire was the subtle hint of untamed sexuality beneath Aline's patrician exterior.

For a couple of days he'd wondered about her sexual orientation, until her stubborn refusal to see him as anything more than a client had given him the first clue to her concealed awareness. Jake wasn't vain, but from the time he'd needed to shave his damned face had proved to be one that most women liked to look at.

His smile assumed a wolfish edge as he followed her up the track. Although she'd tried, she hadn't been able to hide the tiny subliminal reactions that revealed her response. Whenever she'd looked at him her eyes had darkened and colour licked across her pale skin; intrigued, and by that time definitely on the hunt, he'd counted it a minor victory when she'd begun to fix her turquoise gaze on a point just past his head.

He hadn't been able to pursue her because they'd been deep in business discussions, but the long weeks he'd waited out had whetted his appetite.

Now, watching her elegant long legs take the hill, his body tightened in instant arousal when he remembered how they'd felt clamped around his thighs. Desire was the very devil. Perhaps last night shouldn't have happened, but he'd no more been capable of refusing her than he had of swimming the Tasman Sea.

His anger at her rejection was unnerving, indicating just how much her passionate abandon in his arms had clouded his judgement.

If she hadn't made up such a ridiculous story—and yet a couple of times this morning he'd seen a kind of terrified desolation in her brilliant eyes that had made him wonder.

Bitter regret at finally jettisoning a love long past its use-by date?

Or had she really woken this morning with no memory of who or where she was? She was either a damned good actress or some trauma had cut her past cleanly from her.

Irritated with himself because he half-hoped that her outrageous claim was true, he kept a watchful step behind her as they climbed the hill. Not, he thought with a grim smile, that she'd ever ask for help. Even when she'd knocked her head getting out of the helicopter she'd tried to ignore it.

Would such a minor blow to her head combined with what she'd learnt the previous day about her idolised husband have been sufficiently traumatic to give her amnesia?

Or had it been making love with him? That possibility flicked Jake's pride, but somehow this had become no longer a simple matter of an affront to his masculinity, and he wasn't too sure what he planned to do about it.

Nothing at the moment. First he had to deal with the implications of Tony Hudson's concerns about the charitable Connor Trust. Tony might have chosen a better occasion to have confessed that he was worried, but what he'd said at the christening had certainly alerted Jake's sensitive alarm monitors.

He hadn't built his life and his career on making impetuous decisions. He had seven days.

Over the brow of the hill the vegetation changed from heavy forest cover to tall kanuka, feathery and fragrant. As they reached the edge of the trees Aline broke off a small tuft of leaves like soft little arrow heads and crushed them in her hands, then cupped her palms together and inhaled deeply.

'Mmm, I love this scent,' she said huskily, her spine still tingling from Jake's closeness. He hadn't touched her and if she hadn't known he was there she'd never have suspected, because he moved silently and swiftly like a big cat, but her skin had prickled with a primitive acceptance all the way up.

He caught her hands and brought them up to his face. Sensation stabbed her, direct and sinful and compelling. She thought she might always remember this moment, standing on a hill overlooking the sea with Jake's fingers around her wrists, his eyes holding hers.

'Green and fresh and crisply herbaceous,' he said, adding obliquely when she tugged her hands free, 'Almost astringent, yet there's an elusive sweetness underneath it.'

What would it be like if he smiled at her freely, openly, with no hidden emotions or thoughts...?

Too much, she thought grimly. And highly unlikely. This was a man who played his cards close to his chest.

'I thought you wanted to make sure this was an island,' he said.

Until then she'd forgotten her reason for the walk! Feeling foolish, Aline stared around at the wide channel sweeping around the island. Yachts danced over that gleaming blue expanse, and other islands sprawled across it. Some distance away a long peninsula poked out. Squinting into the light, Aline realised that it was covered in a rash of houses.

'Satisfied?' Jake asked, the word a barely concealed taunt.

'This is very definitely an island.' Her voice was deliberately neutral. 'Where are we exactly?'

'That's Whangaparoa Peninsula you can see on the horizon. You live on the south side—the side away from us,' he expanded at her blank glance.

After a taut second he pointed towards the land. 'Keir and Hope live inland just there.' When she didn't answer he looked at her with a twisted smile and elaborated, 'Your boss and his wife, with their baby, Emma, who was christened yesterday.'

Her face froze. 'I see,' she said remotely.

He drawled, 'As if you didn't know.'

It was no use. Tamping down a blast of bitterness, she asked, 'Can we get to the beach from here?'

'If we follow the bush down the valley we'll come out on this side of that headland—the one with the ruins on it.' He checked his watch. 'It'll be half-tide in an hour, so we'll make it if you don't mind scrambling over rocks a couple of times.'

'Not at all,' she returned, walking away rapidly.

He warned, 'It's further than it looks.'

'I'm not a fragile flower.' She tried very hard to use a politely impersonal tone. 'This island doesn't look big enough to exhaust anyone.'

'It's deceptive.'

They talked as they walked along the beach, conversation that was easy and pleasant on the surface although every so often tension snagged them, jagged as reefs beneath the waves. They examined the denizens of the rock pools, even finding a tiny octopus trying to look inconspicuous in the corner of one.

Jake was right; it was further than it looked. By the time they finally reached the house Aline's leg muscles were pulling slightly and she had to force her feet through the clinging sand above the tide line.

'All right?' Jake asked.

'Fine,' she said brightly. Somehow he'd stopped being a stranger and an enemy. Although she'd been resisting him ever since she'd woken in his bed, she was oddly, recklessly glad that they'd achieved this fragile truce. 'It's a lovely island. How long have you owned it?'

The broad shoulders lifted. 'A hundred and fifty years ago there was a thriving little copper mine on the other side, until the sea broke into the tunnels. The first Howard bought it after that. He farmed and fished and gardened; he and his wife raised eight kids here.'

Aline stopped and gazed around. 'It must have been a lonely life,' she said softly.

'With eight children?'

Laughing, she looked up at him. His expression froze. Jerking her chin up, she said, 'What have I done now?'

'Nothing,' he said absently, his eyes hooded against her. 'I like your laugh. It's very pretty. And did you know that when you're angry your eyes go green?'

The comments sliced through her composure. 'Thank you,' she said, falling back on good manners to cover her embarrassment. 'Although I doubt very much whether eyes can change colour.'

'Yours turn green and dangerous,' he said, his voice deep and decisive. 'When we first met I enjoyed your beautiful voice—it is creamy and cool, but always under very tight discipline. Except for that surprising laugh—you slip the leash a bit then. This is the first time I've heard it.'

'Surely not,' she said, genuinely shocked.

'Trust me—I'd have remembered. For a few seconds you sounded young and carefree.'

'Most people sound young and carefree when they laugh,' she returned doggedly.

'Perhaps,' he said, his beautiful mouth curving into a smile that held a cool challenge. A pure gold shaft of light lit up his eyes—an optical illusion, born of the sun. 'Come on, let's go in and have some lunch.'

They ate salad and delicious cold chicken, following it with fruit and cheese. Afterwards, sheltered from the blazing sun, they drank coffee outside beneath the creeper-covered pergola.

When her heavy eyelids drifted down he commanded lazily, 'Go and have a nap.'

'It's such a middle-aged thing to do,' she objected, hiding a yawn.

'Rubbish. It's a sensible thing to do on a day like this.'

His voice deepened. 'Stay here, then. I'll enjoy watching you sleep.'

Not in this lifetime, she thought grimly, struggling up from the lounger. 'No, thanks. I might as well be comfortable so I'll retire to privacy. Besides, I probably snore.' The minute the words left her mouth she knew she'd left herself open to some clever come-back.

He got to his feet too, reminding her again of his size and that effortless, unsettling dominance, the male assurance that challenged her in every way. 'Occasionally you make charming little snuffling noises, but I certainly wouldn't call them snores.'

Fire scorched her skin. She opened her mouth to say something scathing, but had to clamp it shut when her mind remained obstinately blank. Her eyes slid warily past his face and fixed on a point behind his right ear.

'We can't get away from it, memory or no memory,' he said deliberately. 'Last night you made love to me like every man's secret dream, and you slept in my arms with complete confidence.'

Her gaze fell on his hand, relaxed on the back of the lounger. A feverish shiver ran from her fingertips to her spine. That strong masculine hand knew her intimately...

CHAPTER SEVEN

'YOU want me almost as much as I want you,' Jake told her bluntly. A cynical smile curved his beautiful mouth. 'Don't look so horrified—I can control my libido. I'm not going to leap on you from behind a door in the middle of the night and force you to submit to me.'

'I do *not* want this,' Aline muttered inanely, and headed blindly past him.

An outstretched arm barred her way. She lifted her head, defiantly meeting smoky, intense eyes as he trailed his fingertips across her cheekbone and on to her earlobe. Light—so light she barely felt it—yet his touch sizzled through her body, igniting cells, inflaming nerves, robbing her of the ability to think, to talk, to do anything but ache with a clamorous desire.

'Such pretty ears,' he said softly. 'One day, when your memory comes back, I'll buy diamonds for each one, and make love to you while you're wearing them.'

Battered by a storm of passionate recklessness, Aline froze.

'And nothing else,' he said calmly, stepping away from her.

Aline stared at him, her eyes wide and dazed, then angled awkwardly past him, forcing herself not to scuttle cravenly as she headed for the safety of her room.

Once there, she stripped, pulled a T-shirt over her briefs, and jerked back the coverlet on the huge bed to burrow into the pillows as though she might find in them the memories she so desperately craved.

But the only memories she found were those connected to Jake Howard—the scent of his skin, faint yet disturbing, the smooth glide and flexion of muscles beneath tanned skin as he moved, the gilded mystery of inscrutable eyes, and the tawny lights in his black hair...

That way lay danger. Hastily she switched to exploring the dream she'd had just before she woke that morning. She recalled a sensation of overpowering love and comfort, and then a terrible fear as the source of those emotions dissolved.

Apart from that, nothing.

Jake had said she was a widow. Surely if she'd loved a man enough to marry him she'd remember him?

Why couldn't she remember?

A bird screamed outside, a high-pitched wail both familiar and alien. She jumped, then tried to relax, going through a familiar routine of counting and breathing in and out—

She stopped, every muscle painfully taut. How had she known that breathing slowly to a count would ease her tension?

Twisting, she punched the pillows, muttering, 'Because in your brain, behind a very brittle wall, there's everything you've ever done and said and thought and felt. Everything!' Including the previous night, when she and Jake had shared this bed.

Anguished frustration pounded through her.

Desperately she lay back and closed her eyes, repeating to herself, 'I am Aline Connor,' in the hope that the mantra might goad her errant memory.

Eventually she slept, to wake to a dazzle of sunlight and a knocking that had somehow become entwined in her dream—a dream of pursuit, where she searched vainly down dark winding corridors for something she'd lost.

She opened her eyes and sat up, automatically pushing her hair back. Jake stood at the door, his face wiped free of expression so that for a stark, scary moment she saw stamped on his features the ruthless strength that marked a warrior's face.

In spite of the T-shirt, she hauled the sheet tightly above her breasts and eased back against the pillows. 'What do you want?' she asked thinly, shocked anew at his raw male power—and even more shocked at her primal, lawless response.

'You called out,' he said without expression. 'I thought you might be having a nightmare.'

He saw her lashes flick sideways, but he'd already noticed the subtle signs of arousal—darkening eyes, soft mouth, the colour staining her translucent skin. One graceful hand pushed back the tousled hair that stuck endearingly to her cheek, blending the strands into the rumpled jet tresses across her shoulders.

In the plain white cotton shirt she was more intriguing than any other woman in seductive silk or lace, and she got to him as no other woman ever had, packing a punch so hard it damned near unmanned him. Now, when he needed to be able to think clearly, all his subversive brain could manage were erotic memories of her in that bed, in his arms.

She frowned. 'It wasn't a nightmare,' she said, adding awkwardly, 'But thank you for coming to wake me.'

Jake looked at her, his face sombre. Forcing her to stay in this room so that every time she went to bed she'd recall their fevered lovemaking had seemed a good idea, but if she had amnesia it was futile.

If she had it.

For the first time ever he cursed the unreliable mobile telephone link. Cold logic told him a complete loss of memory was highly unlikely, but the sneaking worry wouldn't go away. She had banged her head, even if only slightly, and the previous day had been a traumatic one for her.

Then she'd behaved in a way that was totally out of character, damned near seducing him.

Given her intense loyalty to Connor, Jake wondered grimly if what had been a mind-blowing, addictive experience for him had tipped Aline over the edge, so that the only way to forgive herself for being unfaithful to her husband's memory was to cut him out of her mind.

Jake was beginning to resent just how much that bothered him.

On the other hand, if what Tony Hudson had told him about the Connor Trust was true—and if that long conversation at the christening had roused her suspicion—it was possible she might have a very good reason for pretending amnesia. A large amount of money, enough to mean she'd never have to work again.

When he'd asked Tony if she had anything to do with the day-to-day affairs of the Trust, Tony had shaken his head. 'No, no, but of course she knows what's happening. She and Peter Bournside, the manager, are friends. Very good friends.' Tony's pleasant, honest face had been concerned. 'That's what makes it all so awkward...'

He'd refused to say anything more, but his words stuck in Jake's memory like grit in a shoe.

'Stop staring at me as if I were something nasty washed up on the beach,' Aline snapped belligerently, her eyes glittering green sparks.

'If you think that's how I look at jetsam,' he said evenly, 'you're sadly mistaken.'

Hot colour rushed into her skin again. Glowering, she hunched her shoulders and pulled the sheet up higher, trying to hide. 'Please go,' she said, but her voice wobbled and, to her outraged horror, weak, shaming tears flooded her eyes.

As she twisted sideways and buried her face into the pillow she felt the side of the bed give. Strong, ruthless hands turned her around, and Jake said, 'I thought it wasn't a nightmare?'

She gave a huge gulp. 'Oh, it was all very symbolic! I was looking for something, running and searching, searching and running, banging on doors that wouldn't open. I knew I had to find it because I didn't know where I lived or who my friends were!'

His hands tightened on her shoulders, before sliding around her back and pulling her against his large, secure body. 'It's all right,' he said calmly, his voice very deep and sure.

Beneath her cheek she could hear his heart, slow and regular and infinitely reliable. A sensation of complete trust welled through her—exquisite, unbearable, and as gossamer as moonbeams, because what on earth was it based on?

'I don't know who I am, or who you are. I know the name of the Prime Minister,' she half-sobbed, half-hurled at him, 'and where Australia is—I can see a map of the world in my head. It's all there. But I can't remember anything about me. My life's been wiped out.'

He said quietly, 'Look at me.'

'Why should I?' she muttered, appalled at her complete disintegration. She squeezed her eyes shut, stopping the tears by sheer force of will.

An inexorable hand on her chin tilted her face and held it still. Unable to bear his unseen scrutiny, Aline opened her lashes wide, blazing blue defiance while he surveyed her face with eyes as hard and emotionless as yellow diamonds.

That impersonal, detached gaze hurt her deep inside. She said wearily, 'I don't even remember the man I was married to, and surely I should be able to do *that*. Jake, I want to go back home—I know I'll remember once I'm home.'

'I doubt it,' Jake said absently. 'Your house is like a

nun's cell—nothing personal in it to jog a reluctant memory.'

He appeared to be thinking, his face so empty of all emotion it looked like an austere mask.

Urgently, she demanded, 'Do you believe me?'

His mouth curved in an ironic smile. 'That you've lost your memory? Yes—if only because I know that normally you'd sooner die than let me see you crying, or losing your temper.'

It wasn't the relief she'd thought it would be. Oddly uncertain, she asked, 'Am I so uptight?'

'Not uptight.' In an oddly comforting gesture, he wiped away the tears from her cheeks with his thumb. 'You're controlled, extremely astute. A very cool lady.'

His gentle touch shattered something deep inside her. And because it was dangerous to give in to that pleading hunger for the security of his arms she pulled free of him, surging back against the pillows. 'If I knew *why* I lost my memory I might be able to do something that would bring it back. You told me I'd had bad news...?'

He hesitated before saying deliberately, 'You learned that your husband had been unfaithful to you.'

'Oh.'

Neither spoke. A vagrant breeze off the ocean, fragrant with the promise of unknown destinations beyond the horizon, caressed her pale cheeks. Aline turned this new piece of information over in her mind, examining it with an appalled, sombre intensity.

Why had her husband betrayed her? What sort of marriage had they had? Had she been broken-hearted, or bitter, or furious? Or all three? However harrowing, any emotion would be better than this enveloping blankness.

Eventually she confessed, 'Apart from a kind of regret— the sort of thing you'd feel for an acquaintance if you were told about it—it doesn't mean anything.' She wiped foolish tears away with the backs of her hands.

'It did yesterday.' He got to his feet and stood by the side of the bed, still watching her with that searching gaze.

'Enough to make me want to forget him?' Aline asked, grateful for her T-shirt.

'Perhaps. If you combine it with making love with me last night,' he said coolly. 'That was out of character. I assumed you needed reassurance and comfort.'

'That makes me sound awful—as though I used you!' she exclaimed in distress.

Tawny eyes glinting beneath black lashes, mouth smiling in sensuous reminiscence, Jake laughed deep in his throat. 'If that was how it started, it certainly wasn't how it ended,' he told her frankly. 'I don't know whether you got any comfort from my reaction, but you certainly got all the reassurance about your desirability as a woman that you might have needed. It was one of the most exhilarating experiences of my life watching you come in my arms, untamed and beautiful and erotic as hell.'

Heat stormed through her skin as she recalled the scratches on his back. 'So if I—ah—enjoyed it—'

'You have a talent for understatement,' he interpolated mockingly.

Stumbling but determined, she continued, 'Making love to you wouldn't have slammed that screen down in my brain. It just doesn't make sense.'

'You're a very passionate woman—passionate in your loyalty, passionate in your anger. The combination of your husband's treachery and your desire for another man—and you did want me, Aline, right from the start—could have locked your mind into a conflict that led to this impasse.'

She shook her head. 'It's much more likely that the trigger was finding out about my husband's infidelity.' A wisp of emotion—raw anguish and bitterness—surfaced from somewhere deep inside her. Was that how she'd felt yesterday? Shuddering, she thought that amnesia might have its good points after all.

'True.'

The abrasive note in his voice brought her head around. He was angry, she realised, wondering exactly what she'd said to summon that steely edge of leashed emotion.

Disturbing, enigmatic, he'd been kind in his forceful way. Why, last night, had she decided to make love with him? However upset she'd been, she'd have known that Jake was not a man to take and use and discard.

A desperate need drove her to say, 'Jake, make love to me now.'

His face hardened. 'Why?' he asked.

She bit her lip. And recklessly told him the truth. 'Because I can't look at you without wanting you,' she whispered. 'The only thing that's stopped me from panicking today is that you're here with me. I can't remember making love with you, and I want to.'

The only security she knew was in his arms. It could have been because she remembered nobody else, but she suspected the real reason was that she'd spent the past two months falling in love with him. Something had kept them apart; this might be all she had of him, these days when whatever kept her distant from him had no power over her.

Jake thought he might have been able to resist her if he hadn't already held her fragrant slenderness in his arms, if she hadn't looked up at him with that mixture of shy passion and fear.

Instinct—the deeply rooted need to make her his in every way there was—warred with the need to go carefully in case he made things worse.

What she wanted was security. He wanted so much more from her.

She made love with you last night, temptation purred. A deep, powerful, possessive pleasure sharpened his hunger; although she'd lost everything else, she hadn't lost that. He'd watched her fight her response to him since she'd woken that morning—just as he'd been fighting this slow burn of need, a need that had grown instead of being eased by last night.

'Jake?' she said in a husky whisper that smashed through his will-power, swamping him with a hungry sensuality unlike anything he'd ever experienced before.

He sat on the side of the bed and picked up her hand, surveying its slender, strong length, delicate yet competent. Around the ring finger was the pale line of her wedding ring, the ring she'd hurled from his car.

'Are you sure?' he asked, deliberately expressionless.

She answered directly and fiercely. 'I'm sure. I don't know much about myself, but I understand desire when I feel it. And perhaps...'

His fingers tightened a moment around her hand. With a hard, probing glance he asked, 'Perhaps?'

'Perhaps making love again will give me my mind back,' she said with stark frankness. 'But that's not the main reason.'

Her glance, turbulent and desirous, made the main reason plain. More aroused than he'd ever been before, he wondered why he'd ever doubted her. Memory or no memory, she was honest to the core, and he wanted her so violently that he was prepared to take her any way he could.

Aline's heart lurched at his hooded glance, the golden eyes darkening into arrow points of urgent need. Her breath came urgently through her lips when he stood up and ripped his shirt over his head before unbuckling his belt.

With dilating eyes, she watched the play and flow of muscles beneath his tanned skin as he stripped. Liquid fire gathered in the pit of her stomach, melting her bones and focusing her brain so that all she could see was Jake, magnificent in the quiet room, all she could hear was the thunder of her pulse-beats in her ears, all she could smell was the faint, salty scent that was his alone.

And when he came in beside her all she could feel was the smooth, hot slide of his skin against hers as he wrenched her T-shirt up and over her head, and then she felt his mouth on her breasts, and his hands, and his disciplined strength and his unleashed passion washed over her in a white-hot tide of sensation.

Able only to feel, she let her brain slip into neutral, letting her body take control. She might have forgotten what it was like to lie beneath this man and make love to him, take him inside her, find that forbidden, soaring ecstasy in his arms, but her body remembered!

And her body knew what to do—knew that touching him in a certain way made him drag in a harsh, impeded breath, knew that arching into his taut length made him growl deep in his throat as he smoothed his hands up over her breasts and held her face still to kiss her, thrusting deeply in the sweet reaches of her mouth in a spine-tingling mimicry of what they both knew was coming.

And when it did—when her slick body was begging and she was saying his name in a desperate, driven plea for something—she knew that this was what she had been born for. This man and this moment.

As sensation built, powerful and consuming, the world dwindled to the two of them, the heat and the primal energy of male and female, man and woman, the acute sensory overload until she couldn't bear any more pleasure, would scream if he thrust one more time—and then he thrust, and she screamed and convulsed in an agony of erotic rapture, waves of feeling spreading out from the place where they were joined, rippling like a floodtide through her and on and on.

Jake's breath laboured through his lungs; groaning, he moved faster and faster, and as another tidal wave of ecstasy drowned her she heard his harsh cry when he too reached his peak.

How long they lay together on the ruined bed she had

no idea, but eventually their breathing slowed and he propped himself up on one arm and looked down at her face. 'All right?' he asked.

Aline opened her eyes. He looked like some ancient warrior who'd taken his pleasure of one of the spoils of war. Well, she didn't begrudge him his satisfaction because she felt it too!

'Fine,' she said, her voice hoarse.

'No memory?'

She shook her head. 'It doesn't matter.'

He kissed her swiftly and got up. 'When I heard you cry out I was on my way to check the generator and attend to a hiccup in the pump.' He grinned at her as he scooped up his clothes and went towards the door. 'Give me ten minutes before you try the shower.'

Aline's breath sighed out as she relaxed against the pillows. Her tiredness had disappeared, banished by Jake's potent vitality.

How many other women had made love with him in that big bed? A sudden jealousy pierced right through to her heart.

Don't even go there, she thought wearily as she stretched extravagantly, enjoying the mild ache in her joints.

Jake knew women, and enjoyed them; she should feel gratitude instead of jealousy for the faceless predecessors who'd refined his natural understanding of female sexuality into experienced skill.

Had she learned to love him during the last two months?

'Oh, why didn't my memory come back?' she muttered.

The sun was close to the horizon when she emerged from her room. In the kitchen Jake surveyed her with an amused gaze before indicating a glass on the counter.

'Sauvignon Blanc,' he said laconically. 'Your favourite.'

'Thank you.' Startled by the fierce hit of pleasure at the

sight of him, she made no attempt to pick up the wine glass.

'Unpoisoned,' he said with a faintly mocking smile. 'No drugs, Aline.'

She flushed, but retorted, 'You can hardly blame me.'

'It was an interesting idea,' he said, and opened the door into a pantry, bending to collect a handful of new potatoes. 'Just not my style.'

Well, no. Jake Howard wouldn't have to drug any woman into making love with him. In thrall to a shiver of remembered pleasure, Aline asked, 'Can I help?'

'You don't cook.'

'I can scrub potatoes,' she said firmly.

He dropped them into the sink and smiled at her, a smile that had probably been melting women's bones since he'd started high school. 'Then scrub away.'

Aline enjoyed working beside him in the kitchen. Scrubbing the small white potatoes was satisfying work, and the sound of them bubbling away in the saucepan was gratifying. But better than that—better than anything—was the feeling of rightness, a hundredfold stronger than before, that she felt at his side.

She was drying her hands when she noticed Jake glance out to sea. Alerted by his stillness, like a hunter sighting a target, she followed his line of sight to a speedboat pounding around the headland in a flurry of spray. Noise filled the quiet bay as the craft roared across the water. Not far out from the beach it slowed and settled down into the water before stopping. A moment later she saw a splash as the anchor dropped into the water.

'Friends of yours?' she asked, staring at the three men on board.

Scanning the boat with a pair of binoculars, Jake said briefly, 'No one I know.'

Aline watched an inflatable dinghy go into the water from the stern; two people got in, one carrying what appeared to be a parcel. The outboard buzzed into life like an irritated wasp, whipping the dinghy sideways in a welter of foam. After a couple of exciting seconds it straightened up and headed for the beach.

'Stay here,' Jake ordered, putting the binoculars back on the divider.

'Why?'

'Because I'm going to order them off,' he said briefly.

Startled by his high-handedness, she protested, 'Can you do that?'

'I can,' he told her. 'If they've got a chart—and they will have—they know I've got riparian rights, so they also know they'll be trespassing the moment they set foot on shore.'

Moving with noiseless ease, and very fast for such a big man, he was gone before Aline had time to think. Although he wasn't running, there was something predatory about him, an intimidating aura of authority that tightened her skin even as she told herself there was no danger, just a scene repeated thousands of times over New Zealand—people landing on a beach.

It was only then that she realised these two men, whoever they were, could get her back home. Charged with adrenalin, she bolted out of the house as the dinghy scraped up onto the beach.

The men got out and walked towards Jake across the hard sand. They looked ordinary and safe. Much safer than Jake.

Not that you'd know he was dangerous—he was speaking coolly, his attitude relaxed, his whole stance one of total self-confidence. Was it only Aline who recognised his cold alertness? She jumped the few inches from the edge of the lawn to the sand, landing lightly, but both men caught the movement and started forward.

Jake swung around, something in his hard face bringing Aline to a skidding halt.

The shorter of the two men made a dive for the boat, straightening up with a camera. Heart pounding, Aline stared mutely as he levelled it at her.

'Go back,' Jake said, his voice quiet and flat, his gaze unwinking.

Driven by an instinct as old as danger, Aline swivelled and ran back towards the house, barely faltering when one of the men called her name. 'Aline! Wait, Aline—we just want to talk to you, get your side of the story. You've been very *close* to Peter Bournside. Do you know he's left the country? A large chunk of Trust money is missing— do you know where it is?' A sudden grunt, followed by an outcry and a splash, cut off the words.

She jolted to a stop, turning her head in time to see one of the men drag the camera from the water and shake it.

Jake said calmly, 'Sorry about that.'

'What the hell did you knock it into the water for? You'll pay for this,' one of the men shouted incredulously.

'Bill me,' Jake said, bored.

Her heart thudding heavily in her ears, Aline shot into the house; once safely out of sight, she grabbed the binoculars.

The two men had started to follow her, but Jake was barring the way, unyielding, controlled and uncompromisingly formidable. Voices rose and fell as the men argued vehemently with him, but it was clear that neither was prepared to go past him.

Aline didn't blame them. Big and inflexible, he looked more than capable of dealing with both of them.

Pulses pounding in her ears, she struggled to hear, but their words were indistinguishable; both men kept looking up at the house, and through the glasses she could see from their expressions and their body language that they'd switched from anger to attempts at persuasion.

She could have told them they didn't have a chance of changing Jake's mind.

Eventually they shrugged. Talking fast, the one without the camera said something to Jake. Horrified, Aline watched his big hands clench at his sides. The journalist must have recognised his danger, because he backed off and scrambled into the dinghy; its engine shattered the silence as it started back towards the speedboat.

Tall and forbidding, Jake remained on the beach, watching as the men clambered aboard. One reached for another camera and began to film; he continued to photograph the man on the beach, the house, the bay, until the speedboat had left as noisily as it came.

Only then did Jake turn and come back up to the house. Although his face was impassive, she could sense his towering anger.

Setting her jaw, she went out to the deck to meet him.

He said grimly, 'I told you to stay inside.'

Angry and embarrassed, she resented the involuntary clutch of response in the pit of her stomach. She swallowed, but said crisply, 'What was all that about? Why are journalists trying to take photographs of me? What was that about money?' Anxiety cracked her brittle poise. 'And who is Peter Bournside?'

'He's the executive manager of the trust fund your late husband set up for at-risk youth,' Jake said casually.

There was nothing casual about his watchful eyes, however.

Aline frowned. 'What on earth were they talking about? Do I have anything to do with the Trust?' A swirling, formless panic began to pool beneath her ribs.

He shrugged. 'Not that I know of.'

'Then why would I be interested in him leaving the country?'

'Why indeed?' Jake said indifferently. 'Come on, I'll feel more confident with you inside. I had to threaten them with harassment to get rid of them, and it wouldn't surprise me if they landed in the next bay and sneaked over the hill.'

When she didn't move he urged her through the doors with an uncompromising hand at her elbow. Although the last light from the sun still spilled in through the windows, it no longer reached the trees behind the house. The lush, green growth now huddled in tangled, gloomy obscurity.

Aline couldn't stop a swift, almost scared glance at the hill. 'Why?' she asked, stopping once she was safely inside. 'It was me they wanted, wasn't it? And they were journalists. What's going on?'

'What is going on,' he said curtly, watching her with a cool assessment that lifted the hairs on the back of her neck, 'is a media witch-hunt. Someone has written a book about your—about Michael Connor. I gather it's a piece of hack journalism by a muckraker out to coax a quick buck from those readers who enjoy discovering feet of clay in their heroes. It's full of innuendo and insinuations. Those men are journalists who want to interview you. It's not likely that they'll be the last.'

She felt the colour drain from her skin. 'Why?' she asked stupidly.

'Because scandal sells newspapers,' he said with brutal frankness. Before she could demand to know what scandal, he went on, 'If they discover that you've lost your memory there'll be a feeding frenzy.' Shrewd eyes assessed her expression with clinical detachment. 'I'm assuming you don't want that.'

'No!' Shivering, she looked up sharply into eyes as unreadable as quartz. 'What did they say? What has this hack writer put in his book that's sent journalists chasing me?'

'I haven't seen it so I don't know.'

She sensed he was holding something back, but his shuttered face warned her he wasn't going to tell her. Of course, she didn't have to accept his decision. 'One said something about money.' She frowned, recalling his exact words. 'He asked if *I* knew where the money was. If I've got nothing to do with the Trust, why would I know anything?'

'I have no idea.' Hard golden eyes searched hers.

Anxiety churning inside her, she said sturdily, 'It doesn't matter. Whatever it is, I'll deal with it.'

'As you've dealt with everything else,' he said, still in that ambiguous tone that contrasted with his assessing, unsparing scrutiny.

She shrugged. 'You either deal with life or you go under.' Emphatically she finished, 'Once I get over this amnesia I'll never complain about bad memories. I'll be grateful for them, however awful they might be; having none is like living in a wind tunnel with nowhere to go and nothing to hold onto.'

'It will pass,' he said calmly. 'Are you all right? You're pale.'

'I'm fine. I just wish I knew—oh, well, I suppose I'll find out soon enough.'

After a keen look he said enigmatically, 'I'm sure you will. Would you like to set the table?'

He seemed—distant, somehow. Yet there was nothing Aline could pin down, no shift in his attitude except for a puzzling neutrality.

Not in his reactions, however. When he looked at her his eyes kindled and his voice deepened, and behind the cool irony of his expression she read a need that matched the hunger aching through her.

Aline spent the rest of the evening in a state of simmering excitement, but when she announced that she was tired and ready for bed, he said coolly, 'I'll sleep in another room tonight, just in case we have any nocturnal visitors. I don't want a camera in my face if I'm in the same room as you.'

CHAPTER EIGHT

RACKED by bitter, corroding disappointment, Aline asked, 'Surely you don't expect those journalists to try a bit of breaking and entering?'

'No.' Jake got to his feet, his face hiding his thoughts completely. 'But close the doors to the bedroom, just in case.'

'Yes, of course. Goodnight.' With a set smile, Aline forced herself to walk briskly and erect away from him, sickened by the bitter taste of humiliation.

Surely he could have come up with a better excuse for not sharing her bed?

Something had destroyed the tenuous rapport between them—and it had happened while he held the journalists at bay. What had they said to him? Her head started to throb, so she took a couple of painkillers, then, white-faced and aching with misery, closed the doors in the bedroom and locked the windows half-open before crawling into bed.

Perhaps it hadn't been anything the journalist said. Perhaps he'd had his fill of her...

Raw with pain and a deep, harsh despair, she lay for hours listening to the silent hush of the waves on the beach, wondering how she was going to endure the rest of the week. Jake's rejection was like a sword-cut to her heart, swift and lethal.

She woke late, to another blue and gold morning. But it was the sound of an engine that drove her from the bedroom to the big main room.

Jake was there, and her heart lifted and expanded, filling her with a giddy, heady feeling that vanished the moment she laid eyes on his forbidding, darkly handsome face. 'More journalists?' she said urgently.

He must have read her apprehension. 'It's the helicopter.'

Unnerved, she chewed her lip. 'The one we came in?' At his nod she asked, 'What's it doing here?'

'It's taking us off the island,' he told her, coming across the room.

Cudgelling her brain into action, she stared up into his impassive face, searching it for reassurance.

'Where are we going?' she asked forlornly, but immediately straightened her shoulders, refusing to surrender to the ever-threatening panic that lurked beneath her surface composure. 'And how did you reach the chopper?'

'I used my mobile phone to call the pilot.'

She turned on him, sudden fury flaming like blue fire in her eyes. 'You said you had no way—'

'I said the reception was bad, and so it is,' he interrupted, mouth compressing into a hard line. 'Yesterday I couldn't get out at all. This morning I could. I also discovered that the journalists who came yesterday are on their way back again. A couple of security men are on the chopper; they'll make sure no one sets foot on the island, so with any luck no one will know we've taken off to Auckland.'

The noise from the helicopter's engines intensified as it settled behind the house, then eased off.

'Auckland?' Aline asked, still panicking. 'Why can't I go home?'

She wanted to cling to him, to feel his arms around her, but he was surrounded by a chilling aura of detachment.

'Your house is too easily staked out,' he said calmly, urging her back towards the bedroom. 'We'll go to my apartment in Auckland—there's a landing pad on the roof, and no chance of any journalists getting anywhere near you. Also, I can get a neurologist to come in and check you.'

'A neurologist?'

He looked at her keenly. 'For your memory loss.'

'Oh.' Feeling stupid, she nodded. 'Yes, of course. All right, I'll be ready in ten minutes.' She ran back to her room.

The prospect of being ambushed by journalists appalled her. Folding her clothes swiftly and neatly into her bag, she decided that once she got to Auckland she'd see what the newspapers were saying about the man she'd married. Something there might trigger her memory, spurring her brain into full recollection.

The apartment was large, and beautiful in the same restrained masculine way as the beach house. Without comment, Jake showed Aline into a bedroom that was definitely a guest-room, although it had its own *en suite* bathroom.

Did he suspect that she was falling in love with him? Because although he'd told her he wanted her beyond reason, and shown her how much beyond reason that was, wanting was not love.

And how did she know that the emotion she felt for him was love? It could be simple dependence. Even hostages sometimes developed intense ties with their kidnappers because of the fake intimacy of their relationship. She had no one but Jake to rely on, so of course she'd become dependent on him.

Yet anticipation, subtle and sparkling, glossed her hidden anxiety—anticipation in spite of his sudden aloofness, because she was here in Jake's home.

After she'd unpacked she emerged warily, finding her way into the sitting-room.

'You look like a cat in a new house,' Jake observed from the window. The building was on the edge of one of

Auckland's low cliffs, overlooking a wide panorama of harbour and islands and peninsulas, and over it all a sky the colour of blue velvet, dimpled with the fuzzy images of stars. 'I should put butter on your paws.'

'I feel a bit bewildered,' Aline admitted, her stomach contracting at the image.

'The neurologist will be here shortly.' His voice sounded casual, but again she had the impression that he was carefully monitoring her reactions.

'I—thank you,' she said warily.

He showed her the book he'd been flicking through. 'If you're still amnesiac when all this fuss dies down—and it won't take the news media long to find something else for their headlines—we'll see what medical science can do. In the meantime, you might find this interesting.'

That off-hand linking *we'll* sent a terrifying wave of longing through her, a longing she couldn't afford to give in to.

He was right—it was time to disengage, set some distance between them. Accepting the book, a hearty tome on psychosis, she stepped away, backing up against a large sofa, saying sedately, 'It's kind of you to offer, but I'm quite capable of coping with it myself, thank you.'

His eyes were very keen and hard. 'You're an independent woman, but at the moment you need all the help you can get.'

'With any luck the amnesia will disappear of its own accord,' she said, keeping her gaze on the cover of the book. 'In spite of—what's happened between us—you've admitted that we're not much more than business acquaintances. Business acquaintances don't usually help each other in their personal lives.'

'I'd help anyone who deserved it,' he told her curtly. 'And if you think we're just business acquaintances, Aline, you've got an odd idea of how business is conducted.'

She bit her lip. 'It takes more than—what we've had—

to turn people into lovers,' she said remotely. How could she be so weak? He had only to say her name and she was instantly transfixed by another wave of yearning, sweet and fiery and powerfully addictive.

'Stop savaging your pretty mouth.' He traced the outline with a sure finger.

Aline felt his touch in every cell in her body. Sheer joy fountained through her, life-giving, erotic—*dangerous*—yet she couldn't move, linked to him by the light pressure of his finger on her skin. Looking at him was like being stabbed by arrows of gold.

'Stop looking at me like that,' he rasped.

'Like what?'

'As though you want me to kiss you...' His hand jerked, then he gave a muffled groan and bent his head.

Lost in incandescent delight, Aline stood motionless as he kissed the line of her brows and the sweep of her cheekbones. By the time he reached her waiting lips she was breathing fast and eagerly, her heartbeats drumming in her ears, that fiery tide of need beginning to heat her like lava creeping from a volcano, deceptively beautiful, infinitely dangerous.

'Say my name.' His voice was deep and abrasive. 'Say it now.'

For some reason she hesitated. Something in his tone worried her—a kind of hard impatience, as though beneath that darkly powerful passion there was anger.

Then she surrendered. 'Jake,' she said huskily, dropping the book in her hands so she could reach up to cradle his face. 'Jake, Jake, Jake...'

She was still whispering his name when he crushed the word—and every thought—into oblivion with the pressure of his mouth.

It was a primal possession, a fiercely territorial kiss that stripped her of everything but the need to give him what he demanded, and take an equal measure from him.

When at last he lifted his head, he surveyed her with gleaming eyes. 'Nothing in this world is ever perfect—we have to make the best of the deal life hands us,' he said roughly.

At the soft peal of a bell somewhere, he said something sharp and raw beneath his breath, then lowered his arms and stepped back. 'That will be the neurologist.'

She hid her flushed cheeks by bending to pick up the book she'd dropped. When she straightened she asked, 'Is there a newspaper here?'

'Are you sure you want to see one?' he asked, frowning.

'Yes.'

After another probing glance, he said, 'I'll get a copy.'

'Thank you.'

When he'd left the room Aline let her pent-up breath sigh out; still dazed by the sheer, primitive passion of the kiss, she stared after him and wondered what had happened then.

It was almost as though he'd made a decision—not one he was happy with, but one he could live with.

If she surrendered to the prompting of her heart, what would happen when her memory returned? Did she dare take a chance on that?

The neurologist, a lean, grey-haired man with amused eyes, did some physical tests, examined the small bruise on her scalp, asked her innumerable questions, and finally told her that she looked fine to him.

'I *feel* fine,' she admitted, 'but why did my memory go?'

'Usually it's because of a head wound, but I wouldn't think that the slight contusion you suffered had anything to do with it. Sometimes it's simply a matter of the brain wanting a holiday.'

Startled, Aline laughed.

Smiling, he continued, 'If, for example, you've been enduring a difficult period of your life, or you're faced with an impossible choice, there may be a temporary loss of memory.'

Seizing on the word, she emphasised, 'Temporary?'

'Oh, yes, I think we can be quite sure it's temporary. It will almost certainly come back of its own accord. And as I'm sure you've found out, trying to force it doesn't help.' He smiled at her. 'You'll probably get flashbacks at first, and then more and more will fall into place. Sometimes it's an instantaneous process. If things haven't started moving in a week or so Jake tells me he'll bring you to see me and we can do some tests. However, I don't think you'll have to wait that long. Try not to worry.'

'I'll try,' she said in a low voice. 'Thank you very much for coming.'

He got to his feet and smiled again, wryly this time. 'Oh, Jake's a force of nature when he wants something done. Thank him, not me.'

When he'd gone, she told Jake what he'd said in a voice that tried so hard to be normal it sounded stilted.

He nodded. 'It makes sense. If you relax so that it comes back when it's ready, it should be easier on you.'

Keeping her gaze fixed on the busy harbour scene below, she forced a smile. In spite of everything, she didn't have the right to devour him with her eyes. 'Jake, what do I do? You talked about negotiations—'

'You're an extremely efficient executive in Keir Carmichael's merchant bank,' he said.

It meant nothing. She said bitterly, 'I won't be much use there with an empty head.'

'Even without a memory your head is far from empty,' he told her calmly.

'Tell me about these negotiations.' Perhaps business talk, devoid of emotion, might force a chink through the wall between her present and her past.

Jake sent her a keen glance, but began to talk. Concentrating on his concise, crisp explanation, Aline relaxed as she realised that she understood what he was talking about, but the whole complicated structure he was describing, the huge amounts of money he spoke of, had no significance for her at all, and her part in it seemed just that—a part played by an actor.

'No good?' he said, startling her with his astute recognition of her motives for asking. 'Pity.'

Did he think she was asking for sympathy? Aline flushed, then noticed the newspaper in his hand. 'Is that the one with the extract?'

'Yes. Come and read it over here on the sofa.'

After a moment's hesitation she went across, every nerve wound as tightly as string around a top, and lowered herself onto the cushions. Her stomach dropped into free-fall as he sat down beside her and gave her the newspaper.

The headline was bad enough: 'Golden-Boy Yachtsman's Secret Life,' it screamed. White-faced but resolute, Aline read every word.

Jake's eyes narrowed as he watched her. He'd hoped to get some indication of whether or not she was lying, but the pale mask of her face defeated him. Even when her mouth tightened it was with distaste at the lurid recounting of Lauren's private tragedy, not shock or pain.

The neurologist had told him she displayed some of the characteristics of memory loss, but had warned that it would take more than a brief interview to be certain.

In spite of Tony Hudson's hint that she might be implicated in the mess that was the Connor Trust—and the sneered insinuation from the journalist on the beach that she was Peter Bournside's mistress—he was almost convinced that she was telling the truth. If she was, then this was the best way for her to read it—with no emotional involvement.

Yet he didn't dare accept her word that she had amnesia. Was he indulging in wishful thinking, letting his cold, logical brain be swamped by a decadent hunger that seemed to have no boundaries? Women were just as capable of treachery as men, and he hadn't reached his position in life by trusting foolishly.

Even as his blood ran heavy and hot, he told himself that it was too early to let his guard down, pushing to the back of his mind exactly what he'd do if she was implicated in the losses to the Trust fund.

When she'd finished reading, she scrutinised the photographs. What was going on behind those wide, intensely blue eyes? He was surprised at the fierce protectiveness that engulfed him—and irritated by a ferocious stab of jealousy as her gaze lingered on the photograph of a young man in yachting gear, his smile exultant and rakish.

'He was very handsome,' she remarked in a precise voice.

If you liked your men boyish and charming, Jake thought sardonically. 'Very,' he said neutrally.

'I suppose I must have loved him,' she went on in a distant voice. 'It all sounds very banal—classic adultery.' She pointed to the end of the excerpt. 'Except for that paragraph, which seems to hint at the possibility of embezzlement from the Connor Trust. I imagine that's why the media is hunting—the suggestion of several million dollars stolen from the people of New Zealand is enough to whet any journalist's appetite!'

A reluctant admiration goaded Jake. In spite of the article's careful language—obviously written with the possibility of lawsuits in mind—she'd picked up the most important bit.

Of course, she might know exactly what she was doing.

Casually he said, 'It's just a throwaway line, probably put there to whip up interest in the book.'

Aline was rereading the article. 'I hope he's got his facts right or he'll find himself defending a libel case.'

Suspicion rode Jake hard. He prided himself on his ability to read people, but he'd never been able to read Aline.

Except for her body's involuntary response, she'd always been an enigma behind her delicate, fine-boned beauty.

That hadn't changed, although he'd learned more about her these past couple of days than in the whole of the two months he'd known her. Elusive, hiding that edge of heat with her ice-cool poise, she'd slid through his defences with the ease and stylish skill of a blade forged in fire and tempered in ice.

What was she thinking?

Her lips compressed. 'It's like reading about a stranger,' she confessed, adding with an oblique smile, 'In fact, at the moment you're the only person I know in the whole world.'

'Poor little girl,' he said mockingly.

Aline hid a stab of pain by frowning at the newspaper. 'No wonder the reporter asked me if I knew what had happened to the money.'

Jake leaned back into the sofa. 'Do you think you might?' he asked almost indifferently.

'I don't think so,' she said quietly, easing away from him and folding her hands in her lap. 'That book you gave me said that an amnesiac's basic character doesn't usually change. I find the idea of stealing money from a charity particularly repugnant.' Hoping desperately that the book had got it right, she frowned.

'Don't worry about it,' Jake commanded, getting to his feet. 'It's a waste of time because you can't do anything about it until your memory returns.'

Not reassured, she smiled blindly in his direction. 'I might wake up tomorrow morning with it intact.'

'Let's hope so,' he said smoothly.

CHAPTER NINE

ALINE opened her eyes to sunlight and the scream of a bird. For an instant she lay frozen in a time warp, but after a heart-thumping moment she sighed and relaxed.

No big, alarmingly sensual Jake beside her, just unrumpled pillows, and outside a gull calling impatiently as it limped along the balustrade around the balcony. And still no memory beyond yesterday morning, but at least this time she wasn't shaking with unreasoning terror.

And the empty bed beside her meant that Jake no longer wanted to make love with her. Trying to ignore her heavy, desperate anguish, she accepted that for her emotional safety she had to follow his lead and establish some distance between them.

Islands were romantic, isolated places where the usual rules didn't necessarily apply. Here, in the ordinary, prosaic world, a pragmatic caution was sensible.

Unfortunately it was too late for her. Mingled with the reckless elation rising inside her was the knowledge that in the past couple of days she'd slipped beyond caution's reach into dangerous, uncharted waters.

'So your mission for today is to learn to keep your distance,' she said grimly.

But when she walked into the kitchen Jake looked up, his chiselled mouth curling into a smile, and her heart executed a peculiar somersault that blocked her throat and drove off every rational thought with a blast of pure, shocking need.

'How are you?' he asked.

'Still minus my life before yesterday,' she said, head held high. Flippantly she added, 'But I do know who I am, what I am, and where I am, which is more than I knew yesterday morning.'

With frighteningly fast reflexes he snared a piece of toast that erupted from the toaster like a clay pigeon.

Still shaking inwardly from her flashfire of sensation and emotion, Aline masked his impact on her with slow applause. 'Well caught, sir,' she said, parodying an English accent.

He bowed and dropped the toast into a rack. 'My housekeeper insists it would be a wicked waste of money to buy a decent toaster as there's nothing wrong with this one, but its days are numbered. If I want exercise I play squash or swim, not leap around catching flying toast.'

'You shouldn't have let anyone unload a shop full of designer utensils onto you,' Aline told him. 'Although they look gorgeous, only a few do the job really well.'

He shrugged. 'The place was ready to move into when I bought it. I've put in a few pieces of my own furniture, but I haven't bothered with the kitchen.'

'No elderly, blackened old frying-pan from your days in the restaurant kitchen?' Aline asked, laughing a little because it was powerfully sweet to stand in the sunny kitchen and talk to him.

'I'm not a sentimental man, and I travel light,' he said, turning on the coffee-maker.

Well, yes. No wife, and apparently no lover. Because this made her entirely too happy, she asked, 'Is this apartment your main base?'

'I live here as much as I live anywhere.' He picked up the tray of toast and carried it through another door into the small dining and living-room he'd called the dayroom when he'd shown her around the apartment the previous afternoon.

Last night after dinner they'd sat in the unlit sitting-room and watched the harbour darken and the lights begin to glow while they talked in a fascinating, free-ranging journey that had both satisfied and frustrated her.

Of course she'd welcomed the chance to get to know him better, but she'd missed the undercurrents, the elemental sexual power-play beneath their previous conversations on the island.

Sitting down at the table, she said, 'Why do you still live here? Your business covers the world, so somewhere central would surely be more convenient.'

'I'm a New Zealander. It's my home and I like being here,' he said evenly. 'Nowadays you can do business all over the world without leaving the office.'

'But you still spend a lot of time travelling.' She reached for her napkin and shook it out,

'I've set up the organisation so that I can cut back on life on the road; from now on I'll be more settled.'

Aline surveyed her plate with false interest. 'What do you plan to do with all that leisure?' she asked lightly.

'Pay a few old debts,' he said in a tone that matched hers.

Surprised, she glanced up. 'Debts?'

'Quite a few people helped me when I started out. I'm going to find a way to repay their faith in me.'

'That sounds very noble.' Michael Connor too had felt the need to pay something back. Perhaps she liked men with a streak of philanthropy in their characters...

His brows rose. 'Nobility doesn't come into the equation,' he said dryly. 'I believe in justice and meeting obligations.'

'It sounds suspiciously like nobility,' she teased. 'How will you do it? Set up a charitable foundation?'

'I'll look at the alternatives.' He changed the subject courteously but firmly. 'You'll have to stay inside again today—your husband's trust and its missing money are still front-page news. And there's an excellent photograph of you on that front page.'

With her morning decision fresh in her mind, she said, 'Still no chance of going home?'

Even before she'd finished he was shaking his head decisively. 'Not unless you want to tangle with the journalists camping at your front door.'

'No!' Controlling the flash of panic, she asked, 'Are they still at the island?'

'Two launches have taken up residence in the bay, both supplied with photographers and journalists who look as though they've settled in.'

Aline's mind flew back to the article she'd read in the newspaper. All appetite gone, she put her utensils down and reached for the coffee, pouring herself a cup. She drank from it, then said, quoting from the newspaper, 'I wonder what happened to "the missing millions".' She added, 'Of course, it could just be a media beat-up without any truth to it.'

'That's what the journalists are trying to find out,' he said, his voice level.

Aware that he was watching her, Aline forced herself to drink another mouthful of coffee, but it tasted bitter and rank. She put down the cup, distantly aware of the slight rattle as her hand quivered. Sombrely she hoped that the real Aline Connor—the woman who lived on the other side of the curtain in her brain—was someone she could respect.

Another thought struck her with sickening impact. Perhaps Jake thought she had something to do with the disappearing money—perhaps that was the reason he'd retreated behind his austere bronze mask.

But why on earth would Jake suspect her? You're looking for excuses, she told herself, excuses for his withdrawal. He's probably just bored with you.

'You're not eating,' Jake said.

The stern note in his voice compelled her eyes upwards to the hard angles and unrevealing planes of his face.

After declaring tensely, 'I'm not hungry,' she rubbed away at the frown between her brows. 'If the extract in yesterday's newspaper is correct, and there are several million dollars missing from the Trust, it will have left a paper trail. It's not simple to lose sight of that amount.'

'Could you "lose" it?' he asked coolly.

'Overseas investment would probably be the best way of getting it out of the country,' she said automatically. 'But two trustees would have to co-sign the cheques, so both those trustees would be party to any theft.'

Jake glanced at her lovely, absorbed face, and silently cursed making love to her. Their passionate union had forged unbreakable bonds between them; whatever happened, he'd never be able to forget this woman.

What was it about Aline—only ever her—that splintered his self-command into useless shards? After talking to Tony Hudson at the christening he should have kept well away from her, but, no, he'd had to act Sir Galahad to her beleaguered maiden, and once he'd spirited her out to the island, in spite of the self-control and inner fortitude he prided himself on, each seductive invitation from her had shattered his resolve into fragments.

And it wouldn't take any more than a smile and a glance from her to shatter it again, he thought savagely.

Stressed by his silence, Aline looked into his handsome, arrogant face. What was going on behind those unreadable eyes? An unexpected, unwanted kick of desire, ferociously sweet, untamed and fiery, shocked her into bending her head and staring at her plate.

'Eat up,' he told her shortly. 'One piece of toast isn't going to keep you going until lunchtime.'

She retorted, 'You seem to spend your time feeding me.'

'Would you like me to feed you properly?'

'I don't think such drastic methods are necessary,' she muttered, trying to crush the lazy sensuality his words summoned.

'Then eat something. You have beautiful bones, but that fine-drawn look is getting a bit too ethereal. Try the strawberries.'

Bemused by the dark voice with its compelling undercurrent, she ate strawberries and yoghurt, then managed to swallow another piece of toast. Jake's incisive, mordantly humorous commentary on world events eased a little of the pressure.

Aline was sure that normally she didn't suffer from an inability to make small talk. And then she smiled cynically. How would she know? Perhaps she habitually spent her life racking her brains to come up with a subject that didn't sound trite or foolish or boring.

'Why are you biting your lip again?' Jake asked bluntly.

Flushing, she managed a shrug. 'I'm so sick of this. At first I desperately wanted to remember, but now I'm beginning to wonder whether I'm better off not knowing, and that makes me feel even worse.'

Jake said curtly, 'Stop beating your brain. It'll come when it's ready.'

Anger and frustration warring for supremacy, she shot to her feet. 'I can't wait,' she said feverishly. 'What am I going to do if I don't know how to work—?'

'Stop it!' Two long strides brought Jake in front of her. He caught her hands and held them still. In a voice that crackled with authority, he said, 'You've got a week off— that's another five days, and by then your memory may well have come back.'

'I'm not *worrying*,' she snarled. Furious at the wobble in her voice, she breathed in deeply, so conscious of his nearness and the flood of response in her body that the last remnants of her composure shattered. 'I'm angry! My brain has no right to go off and make decisions without consulting me! I don't know who I really am, and I feel naked and exposed and vulnerable. I hate it! I want to go home and be me again!' Her voice broke on a sob.

Jake's arms around her were wonderfully warm and strong, but she struggled to get away, terrified she'd betray the consuming need that raged through her, eating away her self-control in a blaze of white-hot urgency.

'Stop it,' he commanded. 'Relax, Aline, you're as stiff as a poker.'

'Don't you dare tell me that things are never as bad as they could be,' she spat, lifting her eyes to meet his.

They blazed with the colour and intensity of golden diamonds. 'I won't,' he said tautly, his jaw rigid as each word fought its way past gritted teeth.

Heat swirled within her, coalescing into a molten pool between her thighs, prickling through her breasts until the nipples stood proud and pleading against the cotton of her shirt. An aggressive joy jolted through Aline. When everything else seemed to be falling apart, they had this sexual chemistry.

It was dangerous, and to him it might mean little beyond the physical, but it was open and honest. Jake's cold, disciplined brain could control his face and his voice, but his body obeyed an older, more elemental law. Hardening against her, tense with barely leashed purpose, it hungered for her in the most basic way.

As she hungered for him.

She collapsed against him and buried her face in his throat as she ran her hand down his side.

'Aline,' he said, his voice deep and thick and harsh.

'Are you going to tell me to stop that too?'

'No, I'm going to tell you exactly what you're risking.'

He did, in language that was explicit without being offensive, using words that tingled through her with dark, compelling passion.

Waiting until he fell silent, she lifted her face and kissed the tanned column of his throat. Huskily she whispered, 'I want you so much.'

His arms contracted about her. His hand found her chin

and forced her face out of its refuge against his throat.
'Look at me,' he ordered in a soft growl.

Aline lifted her lashes and stared into his eyes, blinking
because it was like looking into the sun's inner heart—
violent, all-consuming. Yet even there she saw a darkness,
as though he was concealing something from her.

Before she could react he swore, and said in a voice
stripped of everything but famished demand, 'I can't say
no to you,' and crushed her willing mouth beneath his.

Acute pleasure gripped her, submerged her in a heated
tide; as she returned his kiss her secret places softened and
moistened, preparing for an exquisite surrender and claiming.

That territorial desire wasn't just his. Somehow, in a
time hidden from her and without her knowing it, she had
claimed him. Her fingers flexed and dug into his lean hip,
then climbed higher to search out the taut muscles that
gave him such effortless power. She flattened her hands
across his back, relishing the coil and flexion beneath her
palms as he picked her up.

Fierce anticipation melted her brain, bringing with it a
physical recollection of the slow whisper of heated skin
against heated skin, the scent of aroused male, and, just
for a moment, moonlight spilling across a floor...

And pleasure, as exquisite and erotic as the pleasure
they had shared the previous day. Still sealed mouth to
mouth, she closed her eyes as the world whirled.

Against her lips he demanded, 'What do you want?'

It excited her even more to hear his strained voice. She
forced her lashes up and gazed into his face, its classic
framework stark with driven need; this was a memory
she'd hold for ever, even if she had to journey into hell to
retrieve it. 'You. Where are we going?'

'To my bed.' He gave a tight, wolfish smile that sizzled
the length of her spine. Striding towards the door, he said,

'I'm too big to enjoy making love on the floor or the table. Or even the sofa.'

In the huge bedroom, Jake sat her on the bed and knelt in front of her, long fingers deft as he removed her shoes. Startled, Aline looked down at his head, feverish anticipation drumming through her. The wash of fire across his sable hair set her senses reeling: the way his ears sat so close to his head, the spread of his shoulders—all delighted her. He didn't proclaim his masculine ability with obvious, bulging muscles; instead, his lithe, graceful body signalled smooth, understated power.

An overwhelming realisation clutched her heart, wound its way around and through it, binding it with fetters of steel.

I really do love him, she thought, pale with shock. I've loved him for months—probably ever since I saw him. I don't remember it, and I don't believe in love at first sight, but when I looked into his face and heard his voice something went snap and I knew I was lost.

He looked up, and went as still as a hunter ready for the kill, eyes burning as they scrutinised her face. 'What is it?'

Aline leaned forward. 'You have the most beautiful mouth,' she whispered against his lips. 'I love to look at it, and I love it on me.'

Of course he knew she was evading a direct answer—she saw ironic comprehension in his smile and his eyes—but he let her get away with it. 'So kiss me,' he said, deep and raw.

She did, with lingering intensity, afire with euphoria at the thudding of his heart against the palm of her hand. His mouth hardened and she opened hers to it, shivering as he responded.

She moaned when Jake lifted his head and yanked her shirt up and over, not caring when the buttons popped. Her bra followed immediately, and then his shirt. His face intent and purposeful, he kissed her again, pushing her inexorably back into the pillows until she lay beside him, her hair spread out over the white cotton.

'You are,' he said against her mouth, against her throat, against the soft curves below, 'so beautiful you make my heart shake.'

The last word was breathed against the rosy centre of her breast. Aline's breath locked in her lungs when his mouth fastened onto her nipple. Sensation stabbed her, bucking her upwards as she shuddered at the primeval, mindless pleasure of it.

He looked up, reading her face instantly. A slow, ferocious smile curved his mouth. 'I always knew you could look like this for me,' he said with satisfaction. 'Wild, ravishing, with your blue eyes full of secrets and your red mouth stained with my kisses.'

She grabbed his hair, shuddering again at the silken coolness of it against her hands, and guided his mouth to her other breast, holding him there while his clever, knowledgeable lips took her into a sensuous paradise where all she was conscious of were Jake's hands and his mouth and the hot silken slide of his skin against hers, hurtling her into a violent chaos of bliss.

Dimly she realised she was whimpering, pressing her aching, demanding hips against his and then relaxing them, brazenly telling him without words what she craved.

'Yes,' he said harshly, and pushed down her trousers, following his hands with his mouth, branding her with kisses for eternity.

She fumbled with the fastening of his trousers, astonished when her touch made him take a rough breath. It gave her a heady sense of power; she bent and kissed the skin over his heart, then languidly, using wiles she hadn't known she possessed, licked her kiss off.

Jake muttered an oath and let his breath out in an explosive whoosh; with a cat-like smile Aline wriggled sinuously, so that she could reach his shoulder, and bit delicately into the hot swell of muscle.

He laughed. 'I might have created a monster,' he said in a constricted voice, and did the same to her.

Aline's stomach dropped into free-fall when his teeth closed gently on her skin. Black hair gleaming, mocking eyes heavy-lidded, he made an incredible sound, half-purr, half-growl, that turned her bones to liquid.

Sensation expanded through her, sizzled across nerve-ends, invaded every cell in her body; simultaneously she felt twice as strong as any normal woman, and alarmingly, deliciously weak; she wanted to swarm all over Jake, yet she craved nothing more than to lie pinned to the bed by his big body and yield to the tide of exhilarating, desperate anticipation that washed her further and further away from the shores of common sense.

She stared at him as though she could engrave on her heart the splendid framework of his face, the bronze skin and glittering eyes, the scent of arousal, the way the morning light spread lovingly over his long legs and arms, wide shoulders and narrow hips.

He bore her scrutiny with good grace and a half-smile that affected her so strongly she had to remind herself to breathe.

'What are you doing?' he asked eventually.

'Committing you to memory,' she said fiercely. 'No matter what happens, I'm going to remember this.'

His mouth compressed. 'We'll both remember this,' he promised harshly, and slid two fingers inside her.

An untamed sound that should have shocked her broke free of her throat. Enslaved by that primitive invasion, her body arced up into a bow, demanding and insistent. Her hands gripped his upper arms, fingers digging into the coiled muscles.

'Relax—I won't hurt you,' he said deeply, and claimed her with shattering directness.

Transfixed, Aline offered him everything she was, her breath fighting for release as she surrendered completely to the moment.

Unable to think, she surged upwards to meet and match his possession, using her innate female strength to hold him after each thrust, glorying in his strength and her response until the waves of delight peaked and crashed around her. Thrown into some other dimension, she was dimly aware of another cry wrung from her throat as she crested and flew, her body released by serried ranks of pleasure and rapture and a certain, primal understanding that this man of all men was her mate, the only man who could bring her to this place.

As soon as he heard that desperate groan Jake began to move faster and faster within her. Sensing the final shattering of his control, she forced up weighted eyelids so that she could see his face in his moment of truth. This too, she vowed, she'd remember until she died.

A cold foreboding brushed across her. In Jake's grim face, in his utter sensual absorption, she recognised the basic power and energy of the man; something in her mind shifted, cracked, and she recalled the first time this had happened.

The past and the present crashed together in a seamless meld.

And then Jake moved again, his hands clamping onto her hips. His shoulders gleamed in the morning sun as he thrust again and again, deeper and ever deeper, driving her beyond everything to another peak, another triumph beyond triumph. Together they rose in mindless ecstasy until the only sound in the room was the harshness of their mingled breathing.

He opened his eyes and looked into her, as though he could see beyond the barriers that she'd built with such care over the years. Almost as though he sensed her shock, his arms closed around her and pulled her closer.

Attacked by the clamour of memories, she buried her hot face in his neck, but she couldn't hide from her re-united brain. Everything slotted into place—Lauren's revelations, the flight to the island, even the fall over her shoe after they'd made love the first night.

She said into Jake's throat, 'My memory's come back.'

For several humming moments he didn't react. She was about to repeat it when with one swift movement he jerked her face out of concealment and into the light. Meeting his narrowed eyes was like looking into the heart of a furnace.

'When?' he rasped.

'Just then. I can't believe it happened with no drama— just as simple and ordinary as someone pushing a window open.' And she blushed, because it hadn't been ordinary at all. She'd been suffering the most extreme pleasure a woman could possibly endure without dying of ecstasy.

Crimson-cheeked, she muttered, 'Well, you know what I mean.'

'Just like that?' He spoke dispassionately, and the eyes that monitored her expression were as cold and hard as golden diamonds.

Her skin stung with colour that swiftly ebbed, taking with it that melting inner heat to leave her chilly and be-wildered. 'Yes,' she said stiffly, pulling out of his arms. 'Just like that. The neurologist did say that it could happen. I hit my head twice that day—once on the helicopter, and later, after we—when you were outside looking at the moon. I remember tripping over my shoe. I don't remem-ber getting back into bed.'

Jake lay still on the bed, tanned skin startling against the white sheets. 'So he did,' he said, like a judge summing up. 'How do you feel about your husband's adultery now?'

'Angry,' she admitted, but didn't add that subsequent events had muted the raw knowledge of betrayal. Perhaps this incandescent love was what Michael had felt for Lauren.

'It's odd,' she said slowly, feeling her way in the face of Jake's guarded reaction, 'but for the past two days I was sure I'd be delirious with joy at being able to remember everything again.'

'And you're not?' he said, his gaze very keen and shrewd.

'Yes, of course I am.' She frowned, trying to explain. 'But it's complicated everything. There's Lauren, and then there's that wretched book and its insinuations; Michael was no thief.'

'So what do you plan to do?' Jake asked, pushing himself up into a sitting position.

She said soberly, 'I need to get used to—to being me again.' She needed time to get used to remembering, time to ease the pain in her heart, time to work out how she was going to deal with the tangle of emotions.

He didn't like that. Aline wondered how she knew; for the past months she had studiously avoided thinking about him, so it probably served her right that she'd somehow become absurdly sensitive to everything about him.

However, he let her go, watching in magnificent, unashamed nudity from the bed as she gathered up her clothes and walked deliberately from the room.

When she reached the door he said in a hard, deliberate tone, 'Regrouping, Aline?'

She bit her lip. Without looking at him she said, 'Yes.'

Rustling movements behind her brought her head around. He walked towards her and stopped a few feet away. Hard eyes raked her face as he gave a brief, cold smile. 'You'd better open that door and get out of here if you don't want to be hauled back to my bed.'

Furious at the swift, potent tide of desire that his words summoned—sweet and dangerous and almost irresistible—and more furious because she wanted nothing more than to give in to it and forget everything in the heated challenge of sex, she groped for the handle and blundered out of his bedroom.

CHAPTER TEN

BACK in her own room Aline headed straight for the shower. She'd wanted nothing more than to know who the real Aline Connor was; now, with memories battering her as the water played over her passive body, she tried desperately to empty her mind.

Yet the events that had precipitated her retreat into nothingness—Michael's betrayal, Lauren's tragedy, her own turmoil over her desire for a man she hadn't realised she loved—had almost lost their bitter sting. Jake had taken over the empty spaces of her life and filled them. When she thought of Michael and Lauren it was with resignation and a kind of sorrow for them both.

She'd put Michael up on a pedestal because she'd wanted everything in her life to be perfect, she thought, rinsing Jake off her skin, from her hair, from her mouth, accepting as she did that she'd never be able to cut him out of her heart.

And perfection didn't matter any more; because she loved him, she'd take what she could get without worrying about the past or the future.

A shiver rucked her skin as she recalled the darkly possessive note in his voice when he'd said he couldn't deny her. If only she dared—but her courage shrivelled when she considered the cost. She didn't have what it took to make a man happy; for the long term they wanted warm, loving women, not ice queens with high-flying careers and sharp business brains. Eventually, like the other men who'd claimed to love her, Jake would leave her.

And that would kill some essential part of her.

'What are you?' she asked defiantly, combing her wet hair back from her face with her hands. 'A wimp?'

A *sensible* wimp, her mind retorted smartly.

But oh, the more she learned of him, the more she loved him. And making love to him was utterly addictive. Even now her body sprang to life...

Mind churning, she dressed, then tied her hair back. A quick, almost shamefaced glance in the mirror at the heavy eyes and wanton mouth of her reflection revealed flagrantly that she'd been well and truly loved.

No, that she'd made love—there was a huge difference. Jake had said nothing about any emotional bond between them. For him it was simply sex, hot and hard and good enough to want again.

And don't forget, she thought with a cold clutch of anguish, you've made the running every time.

Back straight as an arrow, she worked her shoulders a couple of times to ease their betraying rigidity, then set her jaw and left the sanctuary of her room.

Jake was in the dayroom, frowning out over the harbour from the wide door onto the deck. Silhouetted against the bright morning, he looked larger than life, a graceful giant of a man radiating power and a subtle, potent menace. Aline's mouth dried as she recalled that first night on the island when she'd seen his dark outline against the moon-silvered sea. What had he been thinking then?

What was he thinking now? Like her he'd showered and changed, and not just his clothes; when he turned she saw the mask again, imposed like an autocratic disguise on the striking features.

'All right?' he asked, eyes watchful.

She nodded. 'Fine,' she said automatically, tension thinning her voice and cramping her stomach.

'I made you another cup of coffee.' He indicated a tray on the table.

'Thank you.'

His mouth twisted. 'It's too late, Aline; we can't go back. I know what happens to you in my arms. We have to deal with the fact that we want each other beyond reason.'

'So?' Her crisp tone hid the desolation inside. He'd spoken of hunger, of need, of wanting—never of loving.

'So what did it mean for you?'

'Great sex.' Ironic that she had the perfect weapon to end this agony of indecision. Men in the market for affairs didn't want embarrassing protestations of undying love; if he knew she loved him he might well decide the whole situation was too much trouble. All she had to do was say, By the way, I love you.

She couldn't do it.

Because she loved him, she'd give him whatever he wanted from her for as long as he wanted it. This time, she vowed, she'd not expect it to last a lifetime. When he got tired of her she'd accept her fate with dignity and control—no clinging, no obligations, no tears.

At least, not in public.

Abruptly and without finesse, she changed the subject. 'Did you keep yesterday's newspaper?'

He looked at her with watchful eyes. 'Yes.'

'I want to reread that article.' The mug trembled in her hand. Still stunned by the hugeness of the decision she'd just made, she drank quickly.

Jake indicated a coffee table in front of the largest sofa. 'It's over there.'

'I'd like to see today's papers too, if you've got them.'

His brows drew together over the blade of his nose. 'Why?'

'That implication that someone's stolen money from the Connor Trust needs looking into,' she returned curtly.

'What's it got to do with you?' Jake asked, pinning her down with his unwinking scrutiny. 'You don't have anything to do with the Trust's financial affairs.'

'No, although I have signing authority.'

His eyes narrowed. 'Have you ever used it?'

She nodded. 'Whenever Tony's away.'

Idly Jake asked, 'How many others have signing authority?'

Silently she denied him the right to ask that question, holding his probing gaze as her will clashed with his, but eventually she said reluctantly, 'Just Tony Hudson and Peter.'

'Tell me about Peter Bournside,' he invited.

'He used to be Michael's manager and agent, and when the trust was set up Michael put him in charge of it.' Made uneasy by something she didn't understand in his attitude, she said, 'If there's any question of irregularity in the accounts I want to know.'

'Why?' he asked again.

Pride laced her words. 'Because Michael's name is at stake. Whatever else he was—or wasn't—he was never a thief. Also, if I'm implicated in anything even slightly dodgy I won't have a future as a banker,' she said bluntly.

It was typical of Jake that he didn't attempt to deny her assumption. Instead he said, 'Keir wouldn't sack you.'

She retorted with irony, 'You know better than that. Mud sticks. Keir's a loyal employer, but he's not going to risk his bank. Not that he'll have to, because I'll resign sooner than put him in that position.' Her eyes returned to the newspaper and her oval chin jutted at a dangerous angle.

The stubborn note in her voice kick-started Jake's temper. She managed to keep him continually off-balance. Half an hour ago she'd been writhing in his arms, so lost to everything but the sensations he'd roused in her that her precious control had been shattered.

Obviously it had meant little; once again she was retreating, erecting a wall brick by brick, still obsessing about her husband and intent on protecting her reputation in the cut-throat world she'd made her own. Jake fought a sense of something fragile and evanescent slipping through his fingers.

Hiding his frustration with ruthless practicality, he asked, 'Why did your husband give you co-signing authority if he didn't expect you to take an active part in Trust financial affairs?'

Aline walked over to the sofa, seating herself with the precise grace that was as much a part of her as her waterfall of midnight hair. She put the coffee onto the table and picked up the newspaper, carefully unfolding it and pretending to scan it. Jake noted the soft rustle of the pages. So she wasn't as confident as she'd have liked him to think. He wasn't surprised when she dropped the paper beside her and fixed him with a cool gaze.

'Michael respected my business skills. The signing authority was just a precaution because of course he didn't intend to die. But he'd have expected me to keep an eye on things.'

'Why didn't you?' Jake asked coolly.

Picking up her coffee mug, she drank from it, her blue eyes shadowed by secrets. 'After he died I lost myself in work; I couldn't bear to deal with anything that had his name. Then I spent a year in Hong Kong, and when I came back I was busy.' Busy negotiating a deal with Jake, and becoming so obsessed by him that she hadn't thought of much else. 'I signed a few cheques whenever Tony was away, but nothing else. Until...'

Words she didn't say hung on the air. Jake said shrewdly, 'Until recently?'

Aline shot him a chagrined glance. 'I signed some last week, as it happens. I'd gone to see Peter because Tony told me that no money has been disbursed yet from the Trust. I asked Peter why.'

'And he said...?'

'That he'd been building the Trust fund so there'd be more to distribute once they started.'

'It makes sense,' Jake said neutrally.

She flashed him an indignant glance. 'To a certain degree, but he wasn't building an asset base! He started to boast about his success and my blood ran cold—he's been taking the most outrageous risks, gambling with the Trust money. But what really made me furious—and scared me—was that I could see he was hooked on the adrenalin rush. He didn't even try to hide it.' Remembered anger iced her voice.

'So what did you do?' Jake asked, watching her with eyes the cold, tawny clarity of an eagle's.

'I told him I was going to contact the trustees and find out why they were allowing this, and he laughed, and told me that I was a proper banker—too conventional, too rigid. He said he'd understood Michael much better than I had because they were both swashbucklers.' She paused, fighting for control before resuming more temperately, 'When I told him that Michael had had a conscience, he laughed.' Colour flaked her skin. 'I suppose he knew about Lauren too. Anyway, as I went to go he asked me to sign some cheques. Which I did, but I was so strung up I can't even remember looking at them.'

Jake shrugged as if that meant nothing. 'And when you contacted the trustees, what did they say?'

'Most of them were delighted at the figures he'd given them.' She grimaced. 'Understandably—he'd just about doubled the original donations.'

'Did you tell them how risky this was?' Incredibly, Jake found he was holding his breath. If she'd told them she was in the clear.

She paused, then said steadily, 'No. I didn't want to make assertions like that without concrete proof, and I knew I'd have to walk carefully—I'm not a trustee, so I have no legal status to change policy. I decided to track

Peter's wheeling and dealing so I could show the trustees how insanely reckless he'd been. He rang me after a couple of days and accused me of trying to undermine his position. Actually, he scared me all over again.'

'He threatened you?' Jake asked in a harsh monotone.

She gave him an astonished look. 'No—oh, no! But from the way he was talking I think he'd convinced himself that he couldn't make a mistake, that he was a magician with a golden touch that would never fail.'

'What did you do?'

She gave another wry grimace. 'We had another blazing row.' When Jake's eyebrows shot up she said, 'He shouted and I was polite.'

'But implacable,' Jake said smoothly, sitting down in the chair opposite her.

'He was putting Michael's dream at risk,' she returned, indignation hardening her voice. 'He's an addict, wheeling and dealing for the excitement. So far it appears to have paid off, but he's going to take a fall some day, and lose the Trust huge amounts of money. Michael would never have countenanced rashness like that.'

Stretching his long legs out, Jake asked, 'How well do you know Bournside?'

Restlessly she got to her feet. 'I thought I knew him very well indeed. He was always at our house; after Michael died he was a tower of strength. I like—liked—him very much. I like his wife.'

Jake leaned back, watching her with hooded eyes, his face impassive. Deliberately he said, 'So what do you plan to do?'

'First I want to find out exactly how much the Trust's assets are worth,' she said, with a grim glance at the newspaper. 'The real figures, not the ones he's fed to the trustees.'

'How?'

'That's the problem,' she admitted 'Now Peter knows I'm gunning for him there's not a chance he'll co-operate.'

Getting to his feet, Jake said thoughtfully, 'I might be able to do something about it. I'll get in touch with a couple of contacts—'

Her hands knotted in her lap. She blurted, 'I don't think it's a good idea for you to get caught up in this, Jake.'

'You have no choice,' he told her calmly, pacing noiselessly across the room. 'I can trace money with the best of them, and I can call on people in my own organisation to help if we need them.'

Baffled, she stared at him. 'I can't let you—'

'Lady,' he said with cool authority, 'you can't stop me.' As she seethed he smiled mockingly. 'Wherever you go, you'll find me ahead of you or half a step behind.'

'Why?' she asked in her turn, wondering what she'd say if he told her that he wanted to help her because he loved her—and knowing he wouldn't.

His broad shoulders moved slightly. 'Call me public-spirited. I contributed to the Connor Trust, and so did a lot of people I know. I'll get all the other newspapers sent up and a copy of that book. The writer might have sources we can tap.'

'The book's not being published until Friday,' she pointed out.

'I can get a copy.' He spoke with such formidable determination that Aline was swept along by it.

She said thoughtfully, 'We still don't know whether any money has actually gone missing. The only information we've got is what the newspaper's lawyers decided it was safe to print. The media have been wrong before.'

'I'd say there has to be something more to the accusation than mere smoke and rumours.' Jake looked down at the headline. 'Although that's sensational, the newspaper itself is pretty reliable.'

Aline frowned. 'But missing money could mean anything—from a loss on the share market to embezzlement on a grand scale.'

'Between us, I'm sure we can find out what this is.'

The strength of his will focused onto her as though she'd been caught naked in a spotlight. 'If it's not just a storm in a teacup,' she muttered. 'According to the figures Peter gave me the Trust is in a sound financial position at the moment.'

'Possibly. I'll set things in motion,' he said.

After he left the room Aline sank back into the sofa, feeling as though she'd been blasted by a hurricane and was now lost in the dangerous serenity of its eye. She picked up the newspaper and stared blindly at the print, wondering what on earth she was going to do. Michael's photograph smiled at her, boyish, charming, determined...

She thought of Lauren's desperate, anguished face, and thought painfully, Oh, Michael, how could you do that to her?

She didn't hear Jake come back in, didn't sense his presence until he asked quietly, 'What's the matter?'

'It's like looking at a stranger,' she admitted painfully. 'How could I have been so blind?'

'It happens,' Jake said shortly.

'I know. Adultery seems to occur in the happiest of marriages.' And why should she be surprised that Michael should have wanted Lauren's lush, warm femininity?

'I doubt if happy marriages are much at risk from it,' Jake said with such cool dispassion that she flushed.

'I thought it was happy,' she said evenly. She got to her feet. 'Which makes me an utter idiot. Shall we start work?'

Later in the day Aline glanced up from the computer. White-lipped, she said, 'Where did you get this information?'

'Contacts,' Jake told her briefly. He got up from his

laptop and came across, leaning so that he too could see her screen.

Aline's heart thudded as his faint, unmistakable scent teased her nostrils. Frowning fiercely, she said, 'This has to come from someone working for the Trust in a position of authority. Who's the mole? And why did he or she start copying all this information and sending it to you?'

He straightened up and stood looking down at her, his brows drawn together, his eyes opaque. 'You don't want to know.'

Something like fear chilled her as she tried and failed to trace a niggling thread of memory back to its source. She chewed on her lip, then said curtly, 'If these figures are correct—'

'They are.'

And he wasn't going to tell her why he was so sure of their accuracy. Aline opened her mouth to demand answers, then closed it again. It could wait until this was over. She said sickly, 'According to this, the Trust's lost eight million dollars since the beginning of the year. Some of that's bad investments. Peter took a hiding with a dot com firm—a fact he didn't let the trustees know.'

Jake said absently, 'That could be what the journalist meant.' His profile, sculpted in angles and straight lines, was boldly outlined against dusky sky beyond the window.

'Possibly, but… There seem to be gaps in the record.' Yawning, she focused on the screen again. 'I'll get some coffee,' she mumbled.

'No coffee,' Jake said. 'You drink too much of that stuff.' He glanced at his watch and frowned. 'We'll give it a rest. Dinner should be arriving any minute and we could do with a drink beforehand.'

Aline blinked. 'I don't .want dinner,' she protested. 'I want to find out what the hell is going on here.'

He touched the keyboard and his computer screen dissolved into a dazzle of starshells. 'Not now,' he said pleasantly. 'You're exhausted.'

Aline noted with an odd detachment that the sun was almost setting over the western ranges that sheltered Auckland city from the wild Tasman Sea. 'This is important to me,' she said grittily.

'You're not going to get far when you can hardly see the figures on the screen.'

Another yawn caught her unawares; she covered it, but Jake held out an imperative hand and said, 'Come on.'

His voice was perfectly steady, but she obeyed the authentic note of command, seething with annoyance at her weakness in the face of his stamina.

For much of the afternoon he had been on the telephone and his computer, calling in favours. The results of those calls had arrived in all the ways modern electronics allow. Each scrap of information had had to be checked and double-checked, and slowly they were building a picture.

'You're cold,' Jake said, closing his fingers around hers.

Aline tried to ignore her body's instant, incandescent response. The unfolding saga of the Connor Trust affected her, but intellectually rather than emotionally. Her love for Jake, unsought and unwelcome, pushed everything else from her mind and her heart. Her brain might tell her that unless she could prove she'd had nothing to do with the mess her career was down the tubes and her reputation possibly unsalvageable, but because of this man she no longer cared much.

Until the day Jake told her he no longer wanted her she was going to forget everything and throw herself headlong into just being with him.

She fixed her gaze on a superb picture on the wall. 'I wonder who told the newspaper journo about possible irregularities in the trust accounts. The writer of that book didn't know anything about them—or didn't dare print anything. He concentrated on the sleaze factor. Poor

Lauren.' Jake's silence prompted her to go on, 'And I'd like to know where Peter Bournside is right now.'

He pushed open the door into the sitting room. 'Why did Connor choose those particular trustees?'

'They had expertise and knowledge of young people—they'd worked in the field.'

'And they all had an almost stupefying lack of financial acumen,' Jake observed caustically.

Aline kept her face averted. 'I should have made sure this sort of thing couldn't happen,' she said in a muted voice. Astonished at how easily the sombre words came, she went on, 'I've let Michael down, as well as all the people who donated money to the Trust.'

Jake slid his fingers up to link around her wrist, setting her pulse racing. 'How have *you* let them down?'

'I should have kept a much closer watch on the Trust's finances.'

'Wallowing in guilt is futile,' he said with cool bluntness. 'What would you like to drink?'

'Lime and soda, please.'

'Is that all you ever drink, apart from too much coffee and the very occasional glass of champagne?'

'When I'm working, yes.' During the long negotiations she'd only ever seen him drink once—he'd had a short glass of whisky with Keir after the deal had been signed. She added, 'Like you, I prefer to be fully in control.'

He acknowledged her taunt with an ironic inclination of his head, then dropped her wrist to go over to a tray that had appeared on a sideboard.

'You have domestic fairies in the apartment?' she asked delicately.

He poured the drinks and handed hers over. 'I got this ready an hour ago. You didn't even see me leave the room.'

The liquid slid down her throat, bubbly and refreshingly tart, just as she liked it. Prudence dictated a safe subject.

She gazed around the big, beautiful room and said, 'This is a lovely place.'

'I'm glad you like it.' He picked up his beer and turned to watch her, his face impassive. 'Did you choose your townhouse?'

She swirled her glass, sipped a little, then told him reluctantly, 'Michael found it. He wanted to live near the sea, and the marina is just down the road. And it's close to Auckland—I can get to work in half an hour even in the rush hour. I'll miss it.'

'You're planning to sell it?' His voice was disturbingly soft.

She'd been shatteringly intimate with him, yet now distance stretched between them and it was getting wider. Vivid eyes, glittering like the fire in the heart of a diamond, stabbed into her, seeking something she wasn't able to give because she didn't know how to satisfy a man like him.

Any man.

She stiffened, aware of betraying catspaws across the surface of her drink. 'Yes,' she said evenly, putting it down and loosely clasping her hands in front to stop their shaking. Hastily she added, 'I've lived there too long—it's time for a change.'

'You don't seriously believe that if we can't track down that other money you'll lose your job, do you?'

Aline finished the glass in one long gulp. 'Would you deal with someone under suspicion for mismanagement of funds?'

'No,' he said with brutal frankness, adding, 'But you aren't.'

She shrugged and walked across to the window, staring out into the dusk. 'Not yet,' she said flatly. 'There'll be rumours soon enough if we can't find out who took it and where it's gone.'

'What will you do if you can't shake the rumours? You've worked damned hard to get to your position.'

Not only that; her career was her life, her tribute to her father. She didn't know what else she'd do. Realising that her response wasn't the desperation she'd expected, she said in a stunned voice, 'I'll be relieved.'

'Relieved?' He spoke in a neutral tone.

Damn, why had she had to let that out? Picking her words carefully, she said, 'I enjoy what I do because I'm good at it, but it was never my first choice. My mother couldn't have more children after my sister was born, so in a way I became my father's son.'

'In other words, your father took his wild eaglet and yoked her to his own dreams,' Jake said, his matter-of-fact tone belied by his hard gaze. 'When did you realise you were living his life, not your own?'

Aline shook her head so vigorously she dislodged a strand of hair. Tucking it back, she said intensely, 'I don't accept that.'

'What was your first choice of career?'

'I'd have liked to be a doctor. I wanted to help people,' she said with grave dignity.

A discreet buzz from the intercom indicated a visitor. 'I'll get it,' Jake said. 'It's probably dinner.'

Aline's eyes lingered on his lean-hipped, long-legged, broad-shouldered figure as he left the room. Since they'd made love this morning she'd sensed aggression smouldering beneath his cool exterior. Heartsore, she wondered if he was regretting that rapturous coupling.

Or if he was already pulling away from someone whose reputation could be irretrievably tarnished.

The buzzer did herald dinner—sent over from a local restaurant, Jake told her as she helped him set it out. It was probably delicious, but Aline ate without tasting.

After the meal Jake didn't object when she went straight back into the office and began work again. He came with her, settling down in front of his laptop.

A couple of hours later she said quietly, 'Jake.'

Instantly he got up and came to stand behind her, frowning at the screen.

'Your mole's come up trumps. There,' she said, clicking the mouse. Anger froze her voice. 'Peter's just sold off a big block of shares, and he transferred that money from the Trust account into a bank account in the Cook Islands.'

Jake's brows met over the blade of his nose. 'What makes you think that's—? Ah, I see.' That sharp intellect had grasped the significance of the sum left in the trust.

'Yes,' she said tightly. 'He's taken out every cent he made for the Trust, leaving the exact amount that was subscribed by the public.'

'And it was transferred by cheque?' The words crackled in the quiet room.

'Yes.' She frowned at the date.

'What's the name of the account?' Jake didn't move, yet energy sizzled through him, as powerful as the sexual energy she knew so well. But this was a hunter's intensity, the persistent, lethal, disciplined power that had taken him to the top. Imprisoned by his intense, piercing gaze, she straightened uneasily.

She told him the name of the account. He said curtly, 'Does it mean anything to you?'

'Nothing.'

Jake asked evenly, 'Who co-signed the cheque?'

The figures danced crazily in front of her as the date loomed large. Dry-mouthed, she admitted, 'It could have been me—the dates are right. It was the day we quarrelled and Peter told me that Tony Hudson was overseas.'

'Tony was at the christening,' he said dispassionately. 'He didn't speak of any overseas trip.'

Afraid that she would see suspicion in his eyes, she lifted a proud chin. 'I know. I don't sign blank cheques, and normally there's no way I'd have signed one for that amount without finding out what it was for and where it was going.'

'Normally?'

She looked up, meeting unreadable eyes in an impassive face. Colour faded from her skin. 'I told you, I was too angry with him—too busy arguing—to take much notice of what I was signing,' she said reluctantly. 'I'd like to say that I'd have noticed the amount, but—it got pretty heated and I was all churned up.'

She expected him to probe further, but after one frowning glance at her he said without inflection, 'That's enough for tonight. Go to bed.'

'But—'

'Go to bed,' he repeated uncompromisingly, and leaned over her and quit the computer.

Aline turned angrily, jerking back as she realised how close he was. She could see the fine-grained skin, the small laughter lines at the corner of his eyes, the burnished opacity of his eyes in their thick lashes.

And then she saw nothing because he kissed her, his mouth hard and demanding and possessive as he drew her up against him. She didn't resist; she wanted nothing more than to stay in the unsafe haven of his arms. But too soon he put her away and smiled ironically.

'You're exhausted, and no wonder,' he said, tucking a wayward strand of hair back from her hot cheek. 'If we go to bed together neither of us will get any rest, so spend the night in your own room. We have a lot of work to do tomorrow.'

All very sensible and pragmatic—and cold-blooded. As she walked down the hall to her room Aline thought bleakly that she wouldn't care about not sleeping if only she could stay in Jake's arms all night. Clearly he didn't feel the same way.

She woke with a jolt. All was silent apart from the occasional sound of an engine, but something had woken her—ah! The disks. Before they'd gone to bed they should have copied them and hidden the copies. She frowned into the darkness for a few seconds, then sighed. She wasn't going to sleep until it had been done, so she might as well get up and do it now.

Pulling her T-shirt around her, she opened her bedroom door and tiptoed down the darkened passageway. She was almost at the office when she heard indistinct voices, like a television set turned low.

So Jake couldn't sleep too, she thought, and smiled, a secretive woman's smile. Perhaps they could do something about that...

Quietly she approached the door, easing it open so she could surprise him.

The sound of her own name, said in a voice she didn't recognise, froze her to the floor.

'—changed your mind about Mrs Connor?' the stranger asked. 'You were certain she had to be one of the kingpins, if not the one who organised the heist, and now you say she's innocent. There's a strong likelihood she signed that cheque—poor old Tony Hudson's damned near useless, but he says he'd have remembered a cheque for that amount, and I believe him. What happened to make you give her the benefit of the doubt?'

In a hard voice Jake said, 'I didn't say she *was* innocent. I said it's probable.'

Over the incredulous drumming of her heart Aline heard the unknown man say, 'With all respect, Jake, I hope you're not letting a beautiful face get in the way of logical thinking. That's not like you.' His lightly reproving tone held an undercurrent of nervousness.

'I'm still not sure,' Jake said, the clinical detachment in his tone piercing Aline to the heart. 'And I'm not moving until I know for certain.'

'Look, I know we found nothing when we searched her house—you did a brilliant job of getting her out so we could go in there—but you know yourself, absence of evidence doesn't prove innocence. And although you can't prosecute on rumours, they usually have some basis in fact. What could be simpler than for her to sign the cheque and then split the money with Bournside? Or they could have fun with it together. He's definitely left his wife.'

There was a silence. Aline's breath stopped in her throat as her hand clenched on the door handle.

'I've said it's a possibility,' Jake said, the indifference in his voice killing something vital and vulnerable in her. 'It doesn't matter, because she's not leaving the country until I'm certain of her innocence.'

'Got a way to keep her here?' the stranger asked with a note in his voice that increased Aline's despairing nausea.

'Yes,' Jake said simply.

'All right,' the other man said, sounding disgruntled. 'I'll take this back to the boys and get them to start tracing.' His irritation dissolved into a chuckle. 'The Serious Fraud Office are going to be seriously furious when you hand the evidence over to them. Why did you decide to do this by yourself instead of letting the cops loose on it?'

Aline pushed the door open and said in a brittle, carrying voice, 'I'd like to know that too, Jake. Why not tell us both?'

CHAPTER ELEVEN

NAKED shock darkened Jake's eyes, but it lasted less than a heartbeat; almost immediately a smile, as aggressive as it was humourless, curled his chiselled mouth.

'Because,' he said deliberately, 'three years ago my secretary donated a large amount of money—more than she could afford—to that fund. Her son hero-worshipped Michael Connor, and when the boy died she gave the money in his name. A few months ago I happened to overhear something that set me wondering, so I made some discreet enquiries.'

Nauseated, Aline realised that she'd been set up. Dredging deep into her reservoir of courage she demanded, 'And?'

'And found just enough smoke to hint at a fire,' Jake said deliberately, watching her with eyes as dense and depthless as liquid gold. 'Lots of interesting juggling on the share market, even more rumours, but nothing concrete until I made a point of talking to Tony Hudson at Emma's christening.'

'What did he say?'

Jake's flat, unwinking gaze measured her response with cold detachment. 'That he wasn't happy with the financial state of the Trust, and that he was worried because Peter Bournside had been very elusive lately. We didn't have a chance to talk properly, but he said that you were involved. And that you and Bournside were very good friends.'

'So you immediately suspected me of conspiring with Peter. Of course I was involved—I told you I'd spoken to the trustees,' Aline retorted harshly, her brain fogged by fury and appalled disillusion. 'What made you take such

an interest in this? And don't give me any rubbish about
altruism. You don't know what the word means.'

Jake looked from her to the man who had risen abruptly
when she'd come in the door. 'Wait outside, please,' he
said pleasantly, but the words rang like steel.

Silently the stranger got up and walked past Aline; she
didn't look at him, would never have recognised him
again. Her whole attention was focused on Jake's ruthless
face. How had she let the male beauty of his classical
features blind her to the driving strength and implacable
power so obvious in its arrogant angles and planes?

She was accustomed to pain, but this was new to her—
an emotional agony that lashed her with such force she
had to grip the back of a chair to hold herself upright.
Compared to it, Michael's treachery was nothing. If she
could have crawled back into the hollow caverns of her
mind she'd have done it then, jettisoning every memory
without a qualm.

When the door closed, Jake said curtly, 'I didn't go to
the police with this because I decided that if there was any
chance of dealing with the situation without involving
them I'd do it.'

Aline astounded herself by laughing. Shocked by the
note of hysteria, she summoned every ounce of her will-
power and curbed her tone into studied scorn. 'When did
it occur to you that sleeping with me might make it easier
for you to find out if I was guilty?'

'Sleeping with you wasn't on the agenda,' he said,
watching her with a merciless, burnished gaze. And added,
unforgivably, 'If you remember, that was your idea.'

Red-hot rage fountained through her, reviving her with
an adrenalin boost. Aware that she couldn't give in to it,
didn't dare shriek her rage and devastation because if she
did she'd lose everything she knew of herself, Aline clung
rigidly to the tatters of her composure.

'Indeed it was,' she agreed with icy self-contempt.

'Lucky for you I was so unnerved by Lauren's revelations that I weakly agreed to your *kind* offer of refuge on the island.'

A muscle jerked in his jaw. He paused before saying abrasively, 'I needed time to find out what had happened. Tony Hudson told me quite clearly and categorically that you were behind every decision Peter Bournside made.'

'He's lying.'

'Someone was lying,' Jake said with biting precision. 'I rang Tony a couple of hours ago and dug a bit further, and he told me Bournside had told them all along that you agreed with everything he'd done.'

Jake had made love to her convinced that she was implicated in Peter's schemes, whatever they were. That heart-shaking passion and the companionship she'd valued just as much were lies, like Michael's protestations of love.

Aline almost ground her teeth together, barely salvaging the control to say, 'But you immediately leapt to the conclusion that I was a thief.'

'You should know me better than that. It was a possibility,' he said, golden eyes half-closed and chilling. 'Losing your memory could have been a ploy to block any probing I might do, especially if you'd realised that Bournside had headed overseas and left you to face the music.' He paused before adding with a whip-flick of contempt, 'And you could have seduced me for reasons other than the ardour you produced so conveniently. As well, your memory loss proved rather selective, and came back with astonishing speed and ease once the news was out about possible embezzlement.'

Stark, soul-deadening humiliation raked Aline with spurs of iron. White-lipped, she sneered, 'I'm astonished that you could sleep with a woman you thought a thief, a liar and a prostitute.'

'That's enough,' he bit out.

'And stupid above all,' she added tautly, determined to

purge herself of pain. 'I even gave you my keys so that you could send somebody to search my house.'

Jake knew how to intimidate. He didn't move, didn't alter by so much as a muscle, but a taut, terrifying silence enveloped her like an aura; she faltered to a halt, and every hair on her skin stood up as he walked silently across to stand in front of her, his gleaming eyes hypnotic, a cynical smile curving his chiselled, beautiful mouth. Aline stood her ground, trying to ignore the sudden kick of panic in her midriff.

'Like stealing cake from a child,' he agreed inimically.

He'd systematically stripped her of everything until now she had nothing left but pride. Welcoming the coldness that crawled through her and insulated her from emotion— a familiar feeling, born on the day she'd found out her father hadn't loved her enough to stay alive with her—she lifted her chin and said icily, 'So how is it that you still think there's a remote chance I might not be guilty? As your minion said, lack of evidence is not proof of innocence.'

'If you tell me you didn't sign that cheque I'll accept your word.'

At first Aline thought she hadn't heard him correctly. She glanced up, met eyes as relentless as an eagle's. 'I can't,' she said bitterly. 'I've been trying to remember whether I looked at those cheques. I don't think I did.'

She could remember slashing her signature across the paper several times, but the amounts were as blank as her mind had been on the island. Before he could say anything she finished, 'But even if I did sign that cheque, it still doesn't make me a thief.'

'It makes it damned difficult to prove that you aren't,' he said evenly. 'Especially as you have a reputation for doing things by the book.' He paused, then added, 'Bournside landed in Frankfurt three days ago, and no one has seen or heard of him since.'

She stared at him, her eyes enormous in her pinched face. 'Do you think I knew about this?' Her voice was a whiplash, rejecting him with a cutting desperation that hid the defeat beneath.

'What I think is not important,' he parried. 'You may well have to stand up in a court of law and deny that you knew about it.'

'Thank you for warning me,' she said tonelessly, and turned away.

'Where are you going?' he demanded.

'As far away from you as I can.' Without looking at him she swung on her heels and walked towards the door. Pain slashed every cell in her body, but she managed to summon enough strength to add thinly, 'I have no plans to leave the country, so you won't have to call on your powers of persuasion to convince me to stay.'

He waited until she was almost there before answering. In a voice that held no expression at all, he said, 'I'll get someone to drive you to a hotel.'

She twisted the door handle, almost screaming when it refused to open. 'Don't bother.'

'Unless you want to fight your way through reporters from all three television stations as well as the newspapers, you'd better let me provide you with an escort,' he said caustically.

'I wouldn't let you provide me with toothpaste,' she flashed back.

'What about ecstasy?' he asked, not attempting to mute the cruelty in his words. 'I can provide you with that any time you want it.'

More agony lanced through her, so ferocious she thought she might collapse. She clung to the door handle, exerting her last shreds of strength to open it. 'It means nothing,' she returned, trying for an indifferent tone and managing, she hoped, detachment.

But he hadn't finished with her. 'It meant something to me.'

'That I'm a good lay?' she goaded, intent only on stopping this any way she could so that she could leave before her dreams splintered messily and noisily all around her.

Coldly he retorted, 'When you decide to give up such cheap indulgences as self-pity and put your pride in your pocket, I'll be here.'

'I wouldn't come to you if you were my only chance of life,' she ground out, making the mistake of turning her head.

He gave her an ironic bow, carrying off the old-fashioned courtesy with style, then walked over to where she clung to the handle, removed her fingers from it and opened the door. The man she'd never recognise again was coming along the corridor.

'When Mrs Connor has packed, see that she gets to the Regent without anyone seeing her,' Jake said indifferently.

Without looking at either man, Aline walked out of the room, out of his life and into a future so empty she couldn't bear to think about it.

'You've got another tooth!'

Emma smiled at her, exposing two small grains of rice on her lower gum and one on her upper.

'Soon you'll be able to bite,' Aline said, dropping a kiss on the floss of baby hair.

'She can already,' Hope told her grimly.

Emma wriggled and beamed before deciding to go to sleep, resting her heavy little head confidingly against Aline's breast.

'You're looking more and more like death with each week that goes past,' Hope remarked. 'Why don't you go and get everything straightened out?'

Aline shook her head. To her astonishment she'd confided her emotional turmoil to Keir's worried wife almost a month after she'd stormed out of Jake's life. None of her other friends would have understood like Hope, who'd had to fight her own demons of mistrust and disillusionment on her way to her radiant, enviable happiness with Keir.

'You're so obstinate,' Hope said crossly. 'All right, waste away like a Victorian virgin. For heaven's sake, it was an entirely natural assumption on his part! You'd have thought the same if the situation had been reversed.'

'I know.'

'You're in love with him.'

Aline opened her mouth to deny it, then nodded abruptly.

Her hostess looked at her. 'And you're eating your heart out for him.'

Aline nodded again.

Hope snorted. 'So why—?'

'He doesn't love me. He never did, never made any pretence at it.'

'He must feel something for you!'

Aline said abruptly, 'He thought I'd seduced him to divert him from investigating the Trust. He more or less held me prisoner on the island while he had my house searched for anything incriminating—'

Jerked from her doze by the misery in Aline's voice, Emma lifted her head and looked up worriedly. 'It's all right, darling,' Aline soothed, cuddling her close. She closed her eyes, inhaling the sweet scent of baby flesh and skin.

Trenchantly Hope said, 'He couldn't take his eyes off you at Emma's christening, and I don't think he's a man who lies. He's certainly established your innocence very conclusively.'

'It helped that poor old Tony Hudson remembered he'd signed that wretched cheque as well as me,' Aline said briefly. 'The moment I left Peter he rang Tony and told him he'd just heard of a brilliant investment opportunity, but there was a time limit so Tony had to come in right then and sign a cheque.' She kissed Emma's fat little starfish hand. 'And Tony didn't look at the amount; he said he never did.'

'Did Peter deliberately pick a fight with you so that you wouldn't look too?'

Aline dropped another kiss on Emma's satin cheek. 'He knew *I* wouldn't sign a blank cheque otherwise,' she said dryly, wincing at the way Peter had played on her feelings for Michael to make her so angry she'd neglected her usual precautions. 'But dragging Tony in made the whole set-up too obvious.'

'And of course it was stupid of Peter to be tracked down with millions of dollars in his bank account,' Hope said, adding doggedly, 'Did I tell you that Jake asked me to make sure you were all right?'

'Bad conscience,' Aline said succinctly, shifting on the wide wicker lounger beneath the big magnolia tree. Sunlight slid through the big, glossy leaves to dapple them in coins of gold.

Glowing like a summer goddess, Hope narrowed her amber eyes. 'It was more than that—he was really concerned about you.' Her scrutiny turned shrewd. 'I thought you were still angry, but you're not, are you? You're scared.'

Aline had spent too many dark hours going over every word Jake had said to her, every tiny expression, every smile and frown. Pale now, and resigned, she said, 'This isn't about love, Hope—it's about surrender. He wants me to admit that I can't resist him.'

'Then,' Hope said quietly, 'you're going to have to decide whether or not you'll give him that surrender.'

She ignored Aline's muttered, 'Never!'

'You know, he sounds jealous,' she said thoughtfully.

'Jealous! *Jake!*' Aline snorted.

'Look at it logically.' Hope picked up a glass of orange juice and sipped at it, frowning as she stared at the sun-

dazzled lawn and flowerbeds. 'I'll bet he's jealous of
Michael.'

'He's too confident to be jealous of anyone.'

Hope looked at her. 'Men are vulnerable too.'

'*Jake?*' Aline said again with a hard little laugh. 'When
we made love, he thought I was implicated in Peter's
schemes. He wasn't vulnerable.'

'It sounds as though he couldn't help himself, which
makes him vulnerable too.' Hope leaned forward to say
persuasively, 'Think about it, Aline. You've got two
choices: you can ignore whatever it is between you, or you
can do something about it. Isn't it worth sinking your pride
for? Or are you going to let your fear and that bewildering
inferiority complex block your chance at happiness?'

'You make it seem simple, but it's not. So I go to him;
we start an affair. Oh, yes, that's what it will be,' as Hope
rolled her eyes heavenwards. Aline looked down at the
child sleeping in her arms. 'And then it will fall apart.'

'I didn't know Michael,' Hope said trenchantly, 'but I
think you're making a big mistake assuming Jake is like
him. Jake might be proud and tough and hard, but he's
also honest.' She hesitated, then said, 'Keir likes him and
trusts him.'

'And because Keir likes him he has to be perfect?'
Aline's smile robbed the words of any sting.

'I'd trust him too. Whereas I don't think you trust anyone, not even yourself. You've got so much to offer—
you're extremely intelligent and able, you dress like a
dream, and you're a brilliant friend. Perhaps just a bit old-
fashioned.'

'What?'

Hope grinned at her. 'Nowadays,' she said, 'women go
out and get their men.' She looked down at Emma, sound
asleep, and smiled tenderly. 'Try it, Aline. Believe me,
love's worth any amount of sacrificed pride.'

* * *

Aline lifted a hand to the launch she'd hired to bring her across and set off up the hill, overnight bag in hand. She'd asked the boatman to drop her off on the other side of the island from Jake's bach; now, bag in hand, she clambered up the gully.

After two sleepless nights she was setting out on the biggest gamble in her life, and if Jake sent her away she'd never be the same again.

At least she'd have tried, she thought with sudden passion. She broke off a sprig of kanuka as she passed the trees and sniffed the leaves, remembering the tone of his voice when he'd referred to the underlying sweetness beneath the astringency. Her stomach clenched.

'You can't go back,' she said aloud, tucking the sprig into her buttonhole.

The path down the hill was dry and rocky; she negotiated it carefully, so tense that when a cicada called shrilly she stumbled, and had to grab a vine to stop herself from falling.

At the bottom she glanced across at the grassy patch where the helicopter had landed, the thick lawn and the headlands protecting the shimmering waters of the bay. Slowly, pulses hammering, stomach tightened into a knot, she walked across the grass and around the side of the house.

He lay in the hammock on the deck, long body so relaxed that at first she thought he was asleep. Her heart jumped nervously, then swelled. As she climbed the several steps she caught a flash of fire beneath the heavy eyelids and realised that he was watching her.

He didn't move.

Senses unbearably taut, she walked towards him. The shade of the overhang swallowed her up and for a moment she stood still as her eyes adjusted.

'Hello, Jake,' she said, so relieved when the words came

out sounding normal that she couldn't say any more, just dumped the bag on the deck.

'Aline.' He lifted his lashes and surveyed her with golden eyes as cold and predatory as those of a hunting lion. 'To what do I owe the honour of this visit?'

'You told me,' Aline said deliberately, her voice not quite shutting out the jerky thudding of her pulse, 'that if I wanted you I'd have to put my pride in my pocket and come to you.' She spread out her hands. 'So here I am.'

Jake gave an enigmatic smile and linked his hands behind his head. 'I don't see much evidence of abandoned pride,' he said coolly. 'Your head's still held high, there's still a faintly bored expression on that lovely, patrician face.'

Bored? That wasn't boredom, that was terror. But she didn't blame him for wanting his pound of flesh. 'Oh, the pride has been suitably disciplined,' she told him. 'Along with everything else.'

His gaze skimmed her bare throat, came to rest on the rapid beat of her pulse at the base. 'Everything?'

'Yes,' she said evenly. 'My memories are safely locked in the past where they belong; I've given up using them as a security blanket.'

His glance sharpened, but to her surprise he accepted her statement at face value. 'So what do you want?'

'You.'

Jake's lashes drooped. 'For how long?' he enquired cynically.

'For as long as you want me.'

'And if I said I didn't want marriage?'

She shrugged, although his question hurt. 'Who's talking about marriage?'

With swift, prowling grace he swung up out of the hammock and came towards her. Stripped of all pretence, all defences, Aline met his smouldering topaz gaze, hearing nothing but the thudding of her heart in her ears.

He reached out and touched her cheek with a careless knuckle before using a fingertip to trace the outline of her mouth. '*I'm* talking marriage,' he said with silky precision.

Fire raced from his finger, sparking and crackling through her in fierce, glorious ravishment. Aline closed her eyes and said hoarsely, 'You don't have to buy me with promises of marriage; you've got what you wanted.'

'Which is?'

She took a jagged breath. More than anything she wanted to run away, but she said sturdily, 'You wanted surrender. Well, I'm here.'

'So you are,' he said softly, smiling. 'And are you going to give me everything I want from you—without conditions, without thought for the future, without memories of the past, without control and shields and inhibition?'

She whitened at the very real determination she read in his hard, handsome face, heard in his deep, autocratic voice, but said calmly, 'Yes. If that's what you want.'

'It is very much what I want.' His hand cupped her cheek in an oddly gentle caress and his mouth twisted. 'But is it what you want, Aline? Because I want more than surrender. I want you to want it too—to long passionately for it, to desire it with a heat and hunger that makes everything else seem unimportant.'

Instinctive rejection darkened her eyes. Jake smiled, and the hand along her cheek slid to the back of her neck, anchoring in her hair. Exerting just enough pressure to tilt her head back so that she was looking into his face, he said in a raw voice, 'I want you to jettison that control you've worked so hard to achieve.'

His hard gaze stripped the skin from her, exposing her shrinking inner self to his flaying scrutiny. She closed her eyes against him.

Cold and merciless as steel, he said, 'So why did you come here, Aline? Am I going to be another Keir—a convenient outlet for your sexual urges, but eminently disposable?'

'Let me go,' she said clearly.

He kissed her, but released her before she could respond to the lightburst of energy his kiss summoned.

Without looking at him she walked across to the railing and looked down at the green grass and pale, warm sand to the serene waters of the bay. Stiffly, she said, 'Keir and I slept together once. It meant nothing to either of us.'

'Only once?' Jake said coolly.

'Only once.' Keir had been kind, but definitely unimpressed, making it quite obvious that he didn't want to repeat the experiment. Even now, after she'd made her peace with both Keir and Hope, she still cringed at the woman she'd been then.

'Why? Mutual convenience?'

She looked down at her hands, saw with detachment that they were clenched into small, serviceable fists. 'A silly mistake by both of us. What else do you want?' she demanded hoarsely. 'Blood?'

He said evenly, 'Something much worse—I want the truth. You've lied to yourself and to me all the time we've known each other. If we're to have any chance of any sort of relationship we need to stop hiding behind lies.'

Aline had to force the words out. 'What lies?'

'That this—force—between us is just sex.' When she swung around it was to see him watching her with a taut, mirthless smile. 'There's no escape; at least admit that you're committed to me.'

Silence, while the blood drummed in her ears and the sea shivered against the sand.

Jake said harshly, 'Just as I am to you.'

Trapped by love, by a shattering sense of her own inferiority as a woman, and torn between disclosure and guarding herself from pain, she hesitated. Fight for him, she commanded. What have you got to lose? Yet her tone was bitterly resigned as she said, 'I've already told you that you've won, if that's what you want.'

'Superficial surrender?' Cool and unsparing, his words cut into her. 'It'll do for the time being, but it's not enough, Aline.'

She snatched a glance at him, quivering at the dark dominance of his face.

He said, 'Why did you take one look and decide you wanted nothing to do with me?'

Dry-mouthed, with her nerves stretched unbearably, she said, 'Because I could see that you'd demand—everything.' Silence echoed around her. She stumbled on, 'And I—I had nothing to give.'

'Why?'

When she didn't answer he said tonelessly, 'Because your heart was still buried with your husband?'

'No!' she shouted. She chewed on the side of her lip. Each word came out slow and heavy as she said, 'I did love him. I loved him very much, and I thought he loved me. He was the first man to know what I was like, and yet he seemed to love me.'

There was a short silence. She sensed she'd surprised him, but when he spoke his voice was level and disbelieving. 'What are you like, Aline?'

'You said it yourself,' she returned unevenly. 'Controlled, focused and aloof. Excellent executive material, but with very little to offer as a woman. Or as a daughter.'

'But Connor saw through that mask to the woman beneath.'

She shrugged, made uneasy by a note in his voice. Dismissively she said, 'It's not a mask, Jake. It's the real person.'

'So why did you come here?' he asked in a tone that blew away her composure and left her naked and unprotected in front of him.

'Because I want you,' she said in a defeated voice.

'You can do better than that,' he said implacably.

She whirled suddenly, cheeks red with rage, eyes glittering. 'All right then,' she said, forcing her voice into some semblance of steadiness. 'I am empty without you. I miss you every minute of the day and all the nights. I can't eat, I can't sleep, I can't even clean my teeth without thinking of you! The thought of never seeing you again terrifies me. Is that enough for you? Is that what you want to hear?'

Not a muscle moved in his face or his big body; he examined her for long, humming seconds, before saying harshly, 'It'll have to do. I want the woman who made love to me with such passion and heart-wrenching abandon that I can't get her out of my mind—the woman who makes me laugh, who cuddles babies with a tenderness that twists my heart, who is honest and direct and kind beneath that glossy armour.'

She almost cried with relief, but managed to say carefully, 'I'm—glad.'

Jake crossed the deck in two long strides and pulled her into his arms, holding her so close that every line of his body was imprinted on her, so close she could hear his breathing, feel it, smell him, and taste his hunger.

Her own need began to surge through her like fire across oiled water, like sunlight pouring over the edge of the world, heating her cold skin and warming her heart, melting her body so that it responded with open eagerness when he kissed her and picked her up and carried her back to the hammock.

This time there was no finesse, no studied skill, no patience. They tore off their clothes and came together in passion and greed and an urgent, consuming fever. Within moments Aline felt the savage sweetness build inside her; she clung to him as he thrust deep and hard and powerfully, and almost immediately she climaxed, her need whetted by deprivation and love and relief.

Jake followed, and as he poured himself into her, giving and taking in equal measures, she heard herself say the forbidden words, the words that would put her so completely in his power that she'd never be free again.

'I love you,' she cried, triumphantly, joyously, not even caring, because all that mattered was him. 'Jake, I love you, love you…'

But afterwards, when the passion had faded to a languid afterglow, she hid her face in his chest, refusing to face what she'd done, the magnitude of her surrender.

At least he didn't gloat.

Eventually he carried her into the house and into the bedroom. Listening to the slowing beat of his heart, Aline wondered vaguely what was going to happen next, but she was too replete, too relaxed—too happy!—to care much.

Once in the bed she said drowsily, 'I've got a bag stashed—'

'We'll get it later. You're exhausted—go to sleep,' he said, his voice reverberating through her.

And she did.

The dream dwindled, evaporating swiftly into warmth and a piercingly sweet delight as she woke. Engulfed by pleasure, Aline turned her head and kissed Jake's warm shoulder, then delicately licked his salty, tanned skin, thrilling as he stirred and woke.

After a few moments of sheer, pure satisfaction she gave in to the knowledge that she had to face whatever the rest of the day might bring, and opened reluctant blue eyes.

Open curtains allowed sunlight to spill into the room in golden swathes. Sparsely furnished in a cool, subtle palette of mellow sand tones, the bedroom looked across a narrow lawn onto a curved beach the exact colour of the tiles on the floor. She knew it so well; for the moment it held all that made her life worthwhile.

'This,' Jake said in a rough, after-sleep voice, 'is what

I'd planned that first morning. To wake up beside you and hold you.' He pulled her on top of him and looked at her with narrowed, lethal eyes. 'But when you stared at me with horror and announced that you'd lost your memory I decided it was your way of reasserting control, which meant that you regretted the whole thing. Even though I was furious, I had to admire your cleverness because it certainly served to keep me at bay.'

'A bit extreme even for me,' she said quietly.

His arm tightened around her. 'Later, when I accepted that it was true, I wondered if making love had tipped you over the edge into a state of psychological shock. Losing your memory meant that you didn't have to remember any loyalty to Connor.' His voice was wry and ironic. 'I was jealous.'

So Hope, bless her, had been right. 'So you believed the journalist when he implied I was Peter's lover.'

'I didn't know,' he said indolently, winding a long black lock of hair around his finger. 'I knew that I should keep my distance, yet when you touched me I lost any sort of restraint, of control, completely. That was when I realised that I felt much more for you than the physical obsession I'd been fighting ever since we met. And when you found out, you looked at me with contempt and such cold, furious rage, and I—it knocked me sideways. I was brutal because I wanted you out of the way while I dealt with everything.'

Looking deeply into his eyes, Aline saw the truth burning in them, clear and stark and uncompromising.

'And now?' she asked, stretching on him, her heart quickening at his body's instant, untamed response.

'And now,' he said deliberately, eyes ablaze, 'we start planning a wedding. I love you. If you hadn't come to me I was coming to you—I was going to woo you.'

'I'd have enjoyed that,' she said, laughing a little, pretending to be disappointed.

His smile was lazy, filled with anticipation. 'I'm enjoying this much more. You're all I've ever wanted, Aline.'

A simple statement. Aline heard the truth in his tone saw it in his eyes. 'I do love you,' she said intensely kissing his beautiful mouth. 'I knew that before I got my memory back—that I'd loved you ever since I'd known you. I think hitting my head twice that day gave my mind an excuse for a little holiday because I needed time without the past cluttering up my thoughts and my emotions to realise that you, and the future, are all that matter.'

He smiled, catching the hands that cupped his face, pulling them across his mouth. Against them he said, 'Dearest heart, I love you too. No matter what happens, I swear—'

She cut the words off with another kiss. Against his mouth she said softly, 'You don't have to make promises I trust you.'

Jake's eyes met hers; in that moment, without a word said, they pledged each other a life of trust and love and commitment.

But before they set out on that life, she whispered against his mouth, 'I love you so much.'

'And I love you—now and tomorrow and next year and for ever. I will never leave you, never betray you like your father and Connor did. Believe it.'

And at last Aline did.

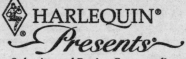

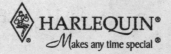

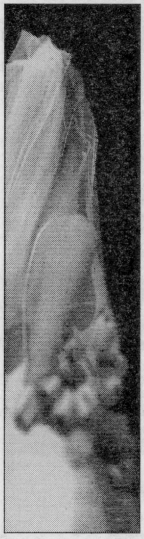